CLOUDS OVER THE VALLEY

Rowan Patrick always believed her mother to have died twenty years ago. Until learning otherwise . . . She goes to the Lake District and finds the Halstead family into which her mother had married after her divorce from Rowan's father. Laura and Chris Halstead are welcoming and explain the calamitous events which severed Rowan's connection with her own mother, twenty years earlier. But Damon Halstead resents Rowan's arrival and suspects her motives in coming . . .

BRENDA CASTLE

◆

CLOUDS OVER THE VALLEY

Complete and Unabridged

LINFORD
Leicester

First published in Great Britain in 1974 by
Robert Hale & Limited
London

First Linford Edition
published 2010
by arrangement with
Robert Hale & Limited
London

British Library CIP Data

Castle, Brenda.
 Clouds over the valley. - -
 (Linford romance library)
 1. Absentee mothers- -Fiction.
 2. Mothers and daughters- -Fiction.
 3. Families- -England- -Lake District- -
 Fiction. 4. Love stories. 5. Large type books.
 I. Title II. Series
 823.9'14–dc22

 ISBN 978–1–44480–033–3

Published by
F. A. Thorpe (Publishing)
Anstey, Leicestershire

Set by Words & Graphics Ltd.
Anstey, Leicestershire
Printed and bound in Great Britain by
T. J. International Ltd., Padstow, Cornwall

This book is printed on acid-free paper

1

'Rowan. Hello there. Are you in? It's me — Kathy.'

The girl clutching the milk bottle pushed open the door and peered into the room; discarded clothing decorated every chair and the breakfast dishes hadn't been cleared away, perhaps not for days. Kathy had never yet seen the flat show any semblance of tidiness, so the scene before her was not unexpected. Nevertheless, it invariably drew a sigh and a feeling of slight irritation, for when Rowan Patrick went out of the house she always looked so neat despite the chaos she usually left behind.

'Rowan, I've brought up your milk,' she said as she came in.

'Thanks,' came an answering voice from the other room which served as a studio. 'I'll be with you in a moment. Make yourself at home.'

1

The flat was situated on the third floor of a converted Victorian house. Kathy Bullen, the first-floor tenant, never entered this flat-cum-studio without marvelling that Rowan Patrick had exchanged her father's luxurious Mayfair penthouse for surroundings so vastly different.

Kathy had once been invited to a party at Louis Patrick's apartment and had been impressed both by it and by Rowan's father, whom she always described as 'dishy' when speaking of that memorable occasion. As for his daughter, she was superbly at ease in this shambles of a flat as in her original home, which was a palatial apartment overlooking Hyde Park.

Rowan appeared in the doorway; her smock was paint-splattered and she was wiping her hands on a rag. She dropped the rag on to the floor, smoothed her fair hair, and smiled at Kathy wearily.

'Thanks for fetching it for me, Kath. I haven't been out today.'

'I thought as much when I saw it

there.' She gazed round the flat yet again. 'I don't know how you can live here after your father's place, Rowan.'

Rowan gave her a smile devoid of warmth. 'I love it here because it's so different. I can deliberately litter this place, whereas it would be sacrilege in Daddy's flat. I hope you don't think I'm a slut by nature, because I'm not. In fact, I intended to have a good turn-out today, only something else came up and I forgot all about my good intentions.'

'Been hard at it, then? What is it this time? Carpet? Wallpaper?' She grinned. 'Or is it a cover for some millionaire's super-loo?'

Rowan laughed. 'It's a book jacket actually, which is something new for me.'

She went back into the studio and Kathy followed her. 'Well, it certainly *looks* interesting,' she murmured as she gazed at it. 'If I saw it on a bookstall I'd definitely look twice.'

'Yes, I feel quite pleased with it myself.' Rowan began to swish her brushes around in a jar of turpentine. 'It's for Steven Llewellyn's new novel. I was lunching with Matthew Carpenter last week and he mentioned that they were publishing the book this autumn so I asked if I could have a shot at doing the cover. Naturally, he didn't like to refuse, but I think it's good enough. He's the type who'd throw it out if it wasn't good, even if I am one of his ex-girlfriends. Anyway, I insist on my work being judged on its own merits.'

Kathy looked at her friend with wide eyes. She never tired of hearing of the rich and famous people Rowan knew, but it no longer surprised her that Rowan, herself, considered such friend-ships normal.

'And is the book as good as Llewellyn's others?' she asked.

Rowan laughed again. 'I wouldn't know. I haven't read it. Matthew didn't consider it necessary. It's a suitably vague design which would suit most stories, and, to be honest, I don't like his work. I'm glad I didn't have to wade through some grim tome I can hardly understand.'

She washed her hands briskly at the sink in the corner and as she did so Kathy became aware of a certain tenseness about the girl she had come to know well in the two years Rowan had lived in the house. Rowan was always relaxed. Her father's wealth obviated a need for her to worry about matters of money, and therefore the world of commercial art was not a cut-throat struggle for Rowan. She only accepted such commissions as interested her, and here again Louis Patrick's contacts made them numerous, although there was no doubt that Rowan's artistic talent was considerable.

As a person, Kathy had always found Rowan easy to be with; she never flaunted her father's wealth to others in less fortunate circumstances. Nothing seemed to worry her, so today the tension was almost tangible.

'I hope you haven't worked on it too hard,' Kathy ventured. 'You look all in, or was it a hectic night last night?'

Rowan wiped her hands with a slow thoroughness, one finger at a time.

'You must be very sensitive to my moods, Kathy. As a matter of fact, I received some pretty disturbing news in the post this morning.'

'Care to tell me?'

'Oh, I don't see why not,' Rowan answered in a tone too light to be true.

She went back into the other room, pulling the smock over her head and depositing it on a convertible settee that looked as if it hadn't been made for days. Then she pulled down her jeans and threw them on top of the smock, adding even further to the confusion in the room. She stood in the centre of the room wearing only a bra and panties and levelled a pair of hazel eyes at her friend.

'Tell me, then,' Kathy urged. 'You and Tony haven't had a row, have you?'

'No, it's not Tony.' Rowan pushed her

arms into a skinny sweater and flicked her hair free of the collar. She indicated with a jerk of her head a letter lying on a table in the corner, amongst a litter of bills and postcards. 'I heard this morning that my mother's just died.'

The silence in the room lasted a mere second or two, but Rowan's last words hung in the air, and it seemed a much longer time. Kathy stared as Rowan stepped into a short skirt. As she zipped it up Kathy said, with a slight shake of her head, 'But didn't you once tell me that your mother died when you were just a baby?'

Rowan's face was expressionless. She went across to a curtained-off kitchen alcove and plugged in the electric kettle. 'Fancy a coffee?' she asked, and Kathy nodded. 'Yes, I'd always believed she died when I was about three years old, but it seems now that until five weeks ago she was a Mrs Delia Halstead. She lived somewhere on the Lancashire-Cumberland border; a place called Skelvingsdale.'

'Your parents must have been divorced.'

Rowan pushed a lock of hair behind her ears. She reached up for the coffee jar and began to spoon the powder into two china beakers. 'Obviously.'

'Gosh. What does your father say about it all? I bet he's furious that you've found out like this.'

Rowan gave a mirthless chuckle. 'Daddy has been in Japan on business for the past three weeks. I had a card from him, funnily enough, this morning. He left Tokyo for Athens the day before yesterday.'

Steam was billowing out of the kettle's spout. Rowan paused to make the coffee whilst Kathy pulled a small table up to the unmade bed on which both girls sat down.

'He's spending the next three or four weeks cruising the Aegean, and then the Mediterranean, in Nico Theoplous's yacht. He'll send me a card whenever he's in port, but, of course, I can't contact him without a great deal of difficulty. Even so, I can hardly put all my questions to him over a radio-telephone, as I could if we were face to face.'

At the mention of the Greek shipowner's name Kathy's mind was suddenly diverted from the disturbing news Rowan had just received. 'Nico Theoplous! How marvellous! They say his yacht is a floating palace. Don't you wish you were going too, Rowan?'

'No,' she answered, smiling wryly. 'I did once, two or three years ago, but never again. He has a daughter about my age, so both fathers thought we could keep each other out of mischief while they got on with the fun. Nico is handsome and charming, but he suffers from wandering hands. Despite my father being aboard, and his daughter, my bottom was black and blue by the end of the cruise. Besides, there'll be quite a bevy of beauties aboard and I wouldn't wish to cramp my father's style.'

'I can't see any female doing that. He's a very attractive man. I could fancy him myself, only he wouldn't look at a poor typist like me when starlets like Belinda Devlin chase after him. No one would ever guess you were his daughter, Rowan.'

'No one ever does. Whenever we go out together, they think I'm one of his girlfriends, and let's face it, Kathy, some of them are no older than I am.'

Rowan frowned, as if she were reminded of the news she had received that morning, and Kathy said, 'How did you find out — about your mother I mean?'

Rowan sipped at her coffee thoughtfully. 'A letter came from a firm of solicitors acting on behalf of a law firm in Kendal. I've been left several pieces of jewellery in her will. I can either collect them from the London solicitors or . . . ' She looked at Kathy and frowned. 'There was a letter enclosed with the official one — it was from a woman called Laura Kingsley. She explains that she was the stepdaughter.'

'How odd,' murmured Kathy. 'What did she want?'

'She just wrote to say that she would be pleased if I decided to call at Skelvingsdale personally to collect the bits and pieces, but if I preferred to collect them through a solicitor she'd understand.'

Kathy put down her mug with an indignant thump. 'It's a bit late for a social call.'

'So it would seem.'

Kathy's face puckered into a thoughtful frown. 'Skelvingsdale? I can't say I've heard of it, but it must be somewhere around the Lake District. I spent a week up there once.' She wrinkled her nose. 'It rained every day. It's been the Costa Brava ever since.'

'I believe it can be very beautiful up there. I've never been to that part of the world. Every other part of the globe that's sophisticated and fashionable, but never there.'

Her voice bore a discernible note of bitterness as she stared unseeingly ahead. 'At any rate, if must have been completely different to the life she spent with Daddy — that's one thing I'm quite certain of. I wonder what happened? I'd give anything to have him here now . . . '

'You'll just have to cool your questions until he comes back.' Rowan looked at her steadily for a moment or two, and Kathy added, 'You don't intend to take up that half-baked invitation, do you?'

Rowan looked away. She finished off the last drop of coffee as if it were a life-saving draught. 'Why not?'

She stared at Kathy again, who said, 'I don't know why not, but I don't think it's a good idea. A woman doesn't give up her daughter for no good reason, nor does a man pretend that his ex-wife and the mother of his child is dead unless there's something not quite right. If she'd wanted to see you, she's had — what is it? — twenty years to do it in. Anyway, she's dead now. This stepdaughter is nothing to you. I think you should wait until you've spoken to your father, Rowan, before you do anything about meeting her.'

'That might be another month, Kathy. I'm too human to wait that long. I'd go crazy just speculating about it, and I can hardly go round asking questions until I've spoken to Daddy.'

Kathy shrugged. 'I suppose you're right. In your place I'd feel exactly the same, only I hope you don't get all emotional over this.'

'Oh, I won't,' said Rowan in that same flat voice. 'I'm just going up there, look them over, which is reasonable enough, and come back. I'd have gone even without an invitation. Anyway, I need a break. I've no work that needs urgent attention now the cover is finished. There's nothing to lose.'

Kathy laughed. 'Only your equilibrium. Why not talk it over with Tony before you finally decide?'

'Tony! I'd forgotten all about him!'

Kathy laughed again. 'A fine thing to say about one's fiancé.'

'He's not my fiancé,' Rowan contradicted. She spoke absently, a frown marring her face. 'I'll have to put off our dinner date tomorrow. I'll ring now. I might just catch him at the office.'

'Why the rush? You're not charging up north immediately, are you? You only heard this morning.'

Rowan focused her attention on Kathy again. 'Of course. I'm going tomorrow, first thing. No time like now to follow up an urge, and I've little else to do that could keep me here.'

Kathy shook her head. 'Well, you're certainly not letting the dust settle beneath *your* feet.'

Rowan shrugged in an offhand way. 'I've had all day to think about it, Kathy, and, believe me, I *have* thought about it. I must go. I don't know what I shall find, and perhaps I won't like all I hear, but I must go.'

Kathy got to her feet. 'Yes, I understand. Well, I shall see you when you get back. I must dash now; I have a date myself tonight. Thanks for the coffee. I'm sorry I wasn't of more help to you.'

Rowan smiled. 'You were, actually. Talking to you helped to make up my mind.'

She made no move to see her friend to the door. She just stared across the room until the door was closed and then she reached for the telephone.

★　★　★

'But this is terrible! Absolutely terrible, and to have to learn it from a solicitor's letter, Rowan!'

Anthony Cherrill looked at it again in disbelief before throwing it down in disgust. 'Why on earth didn't Louis tell you about it when you were old enough to know?'

Rowan shrugged. 'He must have had his reasons, Tony.' She went into his arms and laid her head on his shoulder. 'Don't make too much of it,' she said softly. 'I'm trying not to. I never missed having a mother, you know. Daddy is something of a special parent.'

'All the same . . . '

'All the same,' she insisted, 'don't make too much of it.'

'This woman — this Laura Kingsley — she's got a cheek writing to you *now*. What point is there in visiting them now? There's nothing and no one in Skelvingsdale to interest you any more. If she'd have written two or three years ago it might have been a different matter.'

'I agree, but I'm still going.'

He held her away at arms' length. 'I'd be surprised if you said you weren't going. But consider, Rowan, what would Louis say?'

She bit her lip. 'He'd be furious. I know that without knowing anything about the matter.'

Tony nodded his head in agreement. 'There's absolutely nothing to gain by going there.'

'I'm not sure I hope to gain anything, Tony.'

'She can't have been much of a

mother just to forget you all these years, so why bother? You're not going to get sentimental over this, are you?'

'I don't expect so, but I can hardly tear up the letter and forget all about it. Think how you would feel, Tony.'

He stood in front of the window, his hands clasped stiffly behind his back in a pose that was very characteristic of him. She smiled to herself; Victorian grandfather, she called it.

'My mother is devoted to her family,' he answered stiffly, as if grieved at the implication that she might not be.

'Then try to understand how I feel, *please*, Tony.'

'I am trying, but it all sounds rather unsavoury to me.'

She gave him a bright smile. 'All the better to find out now.'

As she gazed at him across the room Rowan knew then that the attraction he held for her was mainly in his strength of character. Her father was a man of great strength in every way. Rowan believed nothing was impossible for

Louis Patrick, and being his daughter, brought up in the shadow of his powerful being, she automatically sought a man of similar strength in the person she would marry.

She had known Tony a year. He was, she thought, a brilliant architect, having joined a leading city firm some months ago. Coupled with his ability was a burning ambition to succeed. Louis Patrick recognised this in him, a quality he greatly admired in any man, and consequently he approved of Rowan's friendship with the young man. Anthony Cherrill was a young man destined for a great career, and Rowan guessed that he was in love with her, a thought which filled her with delight.

'I shan't be gone above a few days,' she explained. 'I'll be back long before Daddy.' She smiled at him. 'I'm sorry about our date tomorrow night, darling. Can't we go somewhere tonight instead? It will take me only a few minutes to change my clothes.'

He glanced at his watch and began to

cross the room, backing towards the door. 'I only wish we could, but I was almost on my way to Barnes when you called. A local businessman wants to build a sports centre on some land he owns. It will be a big commission, so I'd better get along. No point in keeping the man waiting and antagonising him.'

Almost as an afterthought he came back to her and, pulling her close again, he kissed her. 'When you get back, Rowan, we'll have to discuss our future. I intended it to be tomorrow . . . '

'Yes, Tony,' she answered breathlessly. She had been waiting for months for him to speak of their future together, yet now she said firmly, 'When I get back.'

★ ★ ★

The sky was a dull, leaden grey when Rowan, armed with a road map borrowed from Mr Fiske, a commercial traveller who lived on the second floor, set off the next morning. It wasn't particularly early so, inevitably, she became snarled up in several traffic jams before she was free of London and on the northbound motorway.

The car was a small Triumph, a present from her father on her twenty-first birthday two years ago. He would have had her choose a more expensive model, but, as Rowan had pointed out at the time, a stylish car would look out of place in her neighbourhood, and unnecessary for the small distances she covered.

In the suitcase she had wedged behind the back seat she had put several changes of clothing, for she did not know what lay ahead. The people of Skelvingsdale Hall could, in reality, inhabit a cottage, or, for all she knew, it might be a mansion.

The urge to find out had grown even stronger since Tony had left her the night before. It seemed incredible that her mother had been alive and well for all these years without making an attempt to see her. Her fingers tightened on the steering wheel as mile upon mile of motorway opened up before her. Her father should have told her; whatever his reasons for not doing so, he should have told her she had a mother.

'I had a right to know,' Rowan murmured through tight lips.

Time and time again she had read the letter from Laura Kingsley, and each time she did so Rowan's resentment grew. Her own mother had given her up to look after another woman's daughter, it seemed, and the knowledge hurt.

Her grip on the wheel relaxed. There was a long journey ahead of her; no good could come of building up resentment against a woman she did not know. Rowan decided to treat these few days on her own as a short holiday. Perhaps after she had collected the few pieces of jewellery left to her she would go on to spend a few more days in the area. To relax and return to Tony refreshed.

Somehow there was no urge to rush

back to London, and Rowan was disturbed at the trend of her own thoughts. She knew she should be aching to be back with Tony, for she also knew he was going to propose marriage, which was what she had dreamed of for so long. Only now the importance of an engagement to the man she loved was being pushed into the background of her thoughts by this bombshell exploding so unexpectedly into her life. She knew it shouldn't be so, yet she could think of nothing else but Skelvingsdale and the people who lived there.

* ★ ★

The Triumph cruised along easily at the maximum speed limit permitted by law, and occasionally above it. The radio, with its constant flow of cheerfulness, for once jarred, so she motored on with only her thoughts and the thrum of the engine for company.

The landscape was monotonous. She

wanted only to be at her destination. As she pushed on relentlessly she drove through several showers, stopping only for a quick lunch at one of the motorway cafeterias, and to refill the car's petrol tank.

Her original intention had been to reach Skelvingsdale by the end of the day, but as the day wore on she realised it would, in all probability, mean arriving very late. She was tired too. It was the longest journey she had ever undertaken as a driver, so when she reached Lancaster she drove into the forecourt of a hotel and booked in for the night.

Most of the guests were dressed for dinner and when she approached the reception desk of what was a rather large hotel, the clerk looked askance at her outfit of tight jeans and sweater. But she spoke with quiet authority and the man hesitated only a moment before handing her a pen with which to sign in.

She ordered tea and sandwiches to

be served in her room, after which she climbed into bed, too tired even to think any more. Within a very few minutes she was in a deep dreamless sleep.

★ ★ ★

When Rowan reached Kendall she stopped to ask the way, for Skelvingsdale was not mentioned on Mr Fiske's map. When, at last, she found someone who knew of the village she discovered that she hadn't needed to come as far as Kendal at all.

With the directions firmly implanted in her mind, armed with two strong coffees and some sandwiches before leaving Kendal, she set out once more. The clouds were breaking up by the time she left the town, so she decided to risk a soaking and took down the car's soft top.

It was a relief for her not to be on the motorway any more. She had had more than enough of the soul-destroying monotony of it yesterday. Once clear of Kendal, following the directions carefully, Rowan found herself on undulating country roads which were far more to her taste.

It hadn't occurred to her to inform Mrs Kingsley of her arrival. It didn't seem necessary to let them know she was coming to collect a few pieces of jewellery that in all probability she would never wear. The solicitor's letter had enumerated the contents of the legacy. There had been a gold locket, a diamond and emerald ring and an amethyst pendant. Rowan didn't like jewellery very much and rarely wore the few good pieces she already possessed, so she doubted that she would ever use what her mother had left her.

But she did have a letter of invitation from Laura Kingsley, and Rowan's natural curiosity ensured her acceptance. Besides, a little devil inside her made her curious to catch the Kingsleys (and the Halsteads, if there were any) unprepared.

At the sight of the countryside unfolding around her Rowan soon forgot all else but the beauty of it. She drove down lanes bordered by oaks and beeches which were thick with greenery, and hedgerows alive with the colour of wild flowers that were undisturbed by the vandal hand of man. Rowan knew that no tourist coaches traversed these side roads to which she had been directed.

As the road dipped and soared she caught sight of the sun glinting off many tarns and small lakes. Her rush to reach Skelvingsdale was suddenly forgotten. She stopped at the brow of several hills to survey appreciatively, with the knowing eye of an artist, the patchwork of valley below, more often than not with its shining waters and conifer-clad slopes. And sometimes she would halt for a few moments as the road dipped into a valley to admire the distant fells reaching up into the clouds. Black crags fringed with golden gorse towered above her, cutting her off from the world outside in an awesome kind of solitude of which her present mood made her appreciative.

She passed stone-built cottages and farmhouses sheltered in the folds of the hills. They looked as much a part of the scenery as the abundance of trees all around. The buildings looked as though they had grown there in much the same way.

Hamlets consisting of no more than a few whitewashed buildings huddled together unexpectedly in little valleys, and a multitude of becks shimmered down the hillsides. Where they were deep or wide they were forded by a bridge, often only just wide enough to permit one car at a time to pass.

Blackfaced sheep cropping the lower hillsides still wore their winter coats, and now and again a leather-faced shepherd carrying a stick and accompanied by his dog would pause at the roadside to lift his hat to her as she passed.

Inevitably, she came once more to a

main road — the road she should have taken initially. Rowan knew she had lost some time along the back roads, but the desire to reach the place where her mother had lived and died was no longer urgent somehow. It was more important for her, at this moment in time, to absorb the peace all around.

She drove on for only a mile before a signpost, the first she had seen, pointed down another country lane to the place she was seeking. Where the roads crossed there stood a number of long, low buildings. They were all set amongst screens of trees, almost unobtrusively. Light industry, Rowan thought. The largest of the buildings was the one that had caught her eye. Its grounds were surrounded by barbed wire and there were notices attached to the fencing at frequent intervals to the effect that guard dogs were on patrol at night.

She pulled in to the side of the road and gazed across at the building, which looked something like an open prison.

What had really caught her attention was the name in red perspex over the main entrance to the building — Halstead and Griffin.

There was not necessarily a connection, she told herself, with this place and the Halstead her mother married, although she felt that it might be too much of a coincidence if there was not.

After a moment or two Rowan drove on; she would soon find out.

Skelvingsdale was as pretty a village as she would have wished. Every building in it was old and merged with the scenery in an almost natural manner. The village boasted one inn — The Duck and Gun — one church, and, from what Rowan could see, just one general store. It was at The Duck and Gun that Rowan stopped. She drove the car on to the cobbled car park outside the building and sat there for a moment as she gazed around.

Two women who were passing gazed at her curiously and she guessed that visitors, especially this early in the summer, were the exception rather than the rule.

She got out of the car rather slowly. Now that she had arrived, she was reluctant to take the final step and go to Skelvingsdale Hall. Belatedly she realised that it was difficult to tell from a letter whether an invitation was issued in the way of friendship and genuine welcome, or out of duty. Perhaps it had been a perfunctory invitation; perhaps she would be far from welcome. And perhaps she would be shocked at what she would find at the Hall. Suddenly she was afraid she might discover something horrible about the woman who had given her life.

Indecision tore at her as she stood by the car. The sun was fully out now; it warmed her body, and the air was as fresh as if it had rained heavily all night. Across the road from the inn an old lady sat with arms folded, outside a whitewashed cottage. Her wrinkled face as she watched the newcomer was expressionless. For a moment Rowan had the urge to turn the car around and drive back to London as quickly as she could. Then she brushed back a loose lock of hair and walked slowly over to the inn.

Just as she reached the door the peace was shattered by the noise of a car pulling in behind hers. The very presence of cars in this peaceful village was like blaspheming in church. Rowan hesitated to go into the inn, and instead instinctively turned to see who had arrived. A girl of a similar age to her own got out of the passenger seat. Her hair, which was a few shades darker than Rowan's, was covered with a headscarf and she wore jodhpurs and a man's polo-necked sweater. Beneath it all it was difficult to tell whether she was shapely or not.

The girl glanced at Rowan in a perfunctory way as she crossed the cobbles and went towards a stone archway at the side of the inn.

Rowan wondered if she should ask her way of the girl, but before she could make up her mind a man got out of the car. Rowan wasn't aware that she was staring. Had there been more people about the man might not even have noticed her. But there were only a few yards between them and Rowan in her uncertainty looked to him.

He stared back at her. There was nothing perfunctory about his appraisal of her and she found herself embarrassed as he assessed her. Her jeans were skin-tight and so was her sweater, which barely met the top of her jeans, and she found herself wishing she had slung a coat around her shoulders.

She had worn such clothes on countless occasions and she had been looked at by many men, but never had it embarrassed her as it did now. Usually, mentally forearmed wherever she went, she was never confused by men who looked at her the way this man was looking at her now, but somehow she would not have expected it to happen out here in a quiet little Lakeland village.

The man slammed the door of the car and as Rowan, whose cheeks had reddened considerably, went into the public bar, he turned and followed the girl through the archway.

The landlord came through from the back the moment he heard her enter. He was wiping his hands on a towel and beamed when he saw her, and it was somehow reassuring.

'Yes, Miss, what is it I can get you?'

'A lager, please,' she answered when she found herself breathless. She hadn't intended to have a drink, but her throat was suddenly dry.

'A lager it is, then,' smiled the landlord. 'Just passing through, are you?' he asked as he put the glass on the counter.

'Yes, that's right.' She passed over the money.

'Best time to appreciate Lakeland, before the crowds arrive. You'll be pushing up to Lakeland, I suppose.'

'I thought this was the Lake District.'

'It is, actually, but it's not what the

visitors come to see.'

'I'm just moving around. I haven't any set route.'

She glanced around at the empty room. The furniture gleamed, as did the horse brasses adorning the walls. 'You're not very busy,' she commented.

'Too early. There'll be the regulars in in about half an hour. But then, evening's my busy time. There's a lot of folk farming these parts and they don't always manage to call in during the day. Lambin' season's the worst. I'm always glad when that's over. So are the farmers if it comes to that,' he added with a laugh.

Recognising a man who liked to talk and was in a position to know most people in the area, Rowan said, 'I'm looking for Skelvingsdale Hall. Is it far from here?'

The landlord's eyes narrowed fractionally as his interest quickened. 'Know the Halsteads, then?'

'Not really.' She finished off her drink. 'In fact, I don't know them at all.

I have to see Mrs Kingsley on a small matter.'

'Well, she's a Halstead, isn't she?' he said with a gruff laugh. 'You'll have to follow the road out of the village and take the first fork right. There's no sign, but you'll not miss it because the road's a dead end — leads only to Skelvings-dale Hall.' He hesitated a moment and Rowan deliberately waited. 'My youngest daughter works at Halstead and Griffin. In the office — not the factory.'

'So it *was* a factory I passed down the road. I thought it might be an open prison from the way it was guarded.'

The man laughed. 'Not so open, Miss. They've had security guards since the new laboratories were built. It was never like that when old Mr Halstead was there, nor his father before him.'

'What on earth do they do there to need it so well guarded?'

The landlord shrugged. 'They've always made drugs and chemicals, but when Mr Damon went into the firm he built the laboratories and put in a research team, and the dogs, guards and the barbed wire. My daughter doesn't know what they do; the likes of her aren't allowed into the new part. You need a special pass to get in. There's some that says they're breeding germs for this 'ere germ warfare, but I says, and there's plenty'll agree with me, that no Halstead would be a party to *that*.

'They make drugs, I says to those who are quick to condemn, and you can't risk folks getting their hands on them, not with youngsters being the way they are today. Not that mine would ever take drugs. They don't even smoke.'

He took the empty glass and wiped away the ring it had left. 'Didn't I hear that Mrs Halstead died recently?' Rowan ventured. She made no effort to move. The landlord had proved himself a gossip and, as few people came to the bar during the day, he wouldn't have many people with whom to talk. It was her chance to learn as much as she could.

'That's right. Skelvingsdale Church hadn't been so full since Graham Griffin got married. She was a nice lady, was Mrs Halstead.' He began to polish the top of the bar. 'Caused quite a stir in these parts, though, when she married Mr Halstead. Gave the gossips quite a lot to talk about at the time, and since. What a sensation it was with the divorce in all the papers . . .'

Rowan looked away. No wonder her father had cut that part of his life off completely. How he must have hated the sordid details being made public.

The landlord's eyes narrowed. 'You must know about it, though?' Rowan shook her head and, reassured, the man was only too pleased to continue. 'We all wondered what Mr Halstead was about bringing a woman like that here, but not for long. There wasn't a worthy cause that didn't have her support. She was a real lady and no one can say otherwise. When we crowded into that church it wasn't hypocrisy. She was well liked and respected hereabouts even by those who called her a scarlet woman when she came.

'It just goes to prove that you can't prejudge people. Now Mrs Kingsley'll carry on with the good work where she left off. The second Mrs Halstead did a good job of bringing those three youngsters up. They thought more of her than their real mother.' His face puckered slightly. 'Now Mr Chris is a bit of a wild one — not that he isn't liked too. Mr Damon's got a lot of his grandfather in him. Halstead and Griffin as a firm has provided employment for many people round here, and glad of it they've been. Carolyne Griffin has the stables attached to the inn now.'

Rowan remembered the girl she had seen getting out of the car. 'Is she fair-haired? I think I saw her as I came in.'

'Yes, that'll be Miss Carolyne. Horse mad, she is. The Griffins live over at Barnthorpe; a big modern house. All plate glass. Not my kind of a house, but I heard it cost 'em a fortune to build.'

The door opened and the landlord turned to greet three men who looked, to Rowan, like farm labourers. 'My tongue's always running away with me, I'm afraid. All you did was ask the way, and here I am chattering on.'

Rowan smiled. 'You've been very helpful,' she answered non-committally.

He went to serve the other customers, leaving Rowan alone and contemplative. So, she thought, my mother left me to look after someone else's three children. More than a fair exchange, she thought bitterly.

The landlord came back to her after a moment. 'Now don't forget; drive straight out of the village and take the first turning right. You can't go wrong.'

'I'm sure I shall find it.' She hesitated a moment, undecided, and then asked, 'I wonder if you have any rooms available here? I doubt if I shall stay long at Skelvingsdale Hall, but it will probably be too late for me to move on today. I might want to stay the night and set off early in the morning . . . '

'We keep one single and one double available for visitors. We don't see many, though, even in high summer, so there's usually a room free. There's no need to let me know if you're staying or not. There'll be no call for the room, so it's yours if you want it.'

'Thank you; you've been more than kind.'

As she moved towards the door he said, 'What name is it, Miss? For the room if you do come back . . . '

Rowan bit her lip. Her name would be known. It must still be remembered that Mrs Delia Halstead, before the sensational divorce case, was Mrs Louis Patrick. She turned round. 'The name is Patrick. Miss Rowan Patrick.'

The man just stared at her for a moment. The men at the bar stopped in the midst of their talk of the latest crop sprays to look at her too. She flushed slightly, but was unrepentant. She had nothing to hide and nothing to be ashamed of, and speculating her exact business with the Halsteads would certainly give the inhabitants of Skelvingsdale something new to talk about, she reckoned.

2

The view from the forecourt of Skelvingsdale Hall was of dizzying proportions.
Rowan stopped the car outside the house
and stepped on to the gravel. Whereas
the village of Skelvingsdale lay in a hollow
in the hills, the house from which it
took its name stood atop a hill. Below
lay patchwork fields and a small tarn
which, now the sun had retreated behind
clouds, looked like a slab of pewter.
Miles distant she could see cars crawl-
ing along the main road on which she
had come, and somewhere near, cloaked
by trees, would be the guarded factory
of Halstead and Griffin.

Rowan had left the village according
to the landlord's instructions, following
the narrow road up the hill. The hill
was so thick with conifers that the
house itself, lording it over the surrounding countryside, was come upon

as something of a surprise.

She swung round to examine the house itself. It was of grey stone, early Victorian and, in Rowan's opinion, ugly. A virginia creeper clung to the façade, snaking its way over the closed doorway. No cars stood in the drive apart from Rowan's, and in the few minutes she had spent outside she had detected no sign of human life. The gravel driveway swung round the house, so, she supposed, it was possible that a car was in one of the garages hidden at the rear of the building.

She was about to rap at the brass door-knocker when she heard the sound of a car approaching through the trees. She stood by her car as an American station-wagon drew up alongside. The woman who got out stared at Rowan. Her dog, a black-and-white Border Collie, jumped out at her heels and snapped so ferociously that Rowan stepped back against her car.

'Down, Hamish! Down, I say.'

The dog retreated and the woman

smiled up at Rowan. 'Sorry about that, dear. He's a good watchdog, but quite harmless.'

'That's all right,' answered Rowan. 'I like dogs.' But, nevertheless, she kept her eyes on the animal.

The woman began to take boxes of groceries out of the back of the station-wagon. 'This is my shopping day,' she explained in a rather breathless fashion. 'I take an absolutely enormous list with me, but I always manage to forget something and then I have to go down to the village and fetch it. It's most annoying, but it happens every time.'

'May I help?'

'Oh, would you? That is kind of you. I won't keep you waiting much longer. I just want to get these out of the car and into the house, so Mrs Jennings can put them away. Here you are. Think you can manage that?'

She handed Rowan a basket and hurried towards the house, the dog frisking at her heels. She walked into the house backwards, pushing open the door as she went. Rowan followed her into the hall, where she deposited the basket on an oak table.

'Now,' said the woman, brushing back a wisp of dark hair from a face that was shiny, 'I'm sorry about this, but we don't keep much staff; only Mrs Jennings, who's by way of a cook-housekeeper, and Mary. But these girls don't stay for long. Wages and opportunities in the cities lure them away. We can't compete. Of course, we have Mrs Dowson to do the heavy work, and it's as well. We can rely on her. Chris always says there's a new girl here each time he comes home, which is an exaggeration . . . Oh, dear,' she went on, laughing, 'how I do go on.'

Rowan smiled. It seemed that country dwellers had the gift of garrulity, for the two people she had so far met had hardly paused for breath between words.

'It seems that everyone has the same trouble when it comes to domestic staff,' she answered soothingly.

'Yes, indeed. And I've kept you waiting far too long already. I suppose you've come about the jumble for the bazaar, but I'm afraid I haven't . . .'

'It's nothing to do with the bazaar,' Rowan broke in quickly before the woman started another monologue on some other subject. 'I've come to see Mrs Kingsley. Mrs Laura Kingsley.'

The woman stared. '*I'm* Laura Kingsley.'

Rowan supposed she should have guessed, only she had somehow expected the stepdaughter to be someone who was around her own age. This woman was near to forty, her hair cut into no style in particular, and her clothes plain and tweedy. The face that looked at Rowan was pleasant enough, but Laura Kingsley was a woman who would be easily lost in a crowd.

'I'm Rowan Patrick.'

Laura Kingsley kept on staring as if she couldn't believe her eyes. 'Good heavens!' she exclaimed after a moment's stunned surprise. 'Rowan.'

'I apologise for turning up like this. I should have let you know I was coming.'

Laura Kingsley roused herself after staring mesmerised at the younger woman for a further few moments. 'There was no need, my dear, no need at all.' She glanced frantically around the hall. 'Mary! Mary!'

A girl wearing a nylon overall with dusters crammed into her pockets appeared a moment later. 'Mary, take these groceries to Mrs Jennings and be quick about it. She's waiting for some of these things — and take Hamish with you.'

The girl did as she was told, but not before she had cast a curious look at Rowan.

'Well,' Laura Kingsley said briskly, 'what a surprise. I wrote hoping . . . but I never thought . . . I'm so glad you came. Come along into the living room where we can be comfortable. I've kept you in the hall for long enough.'

Rowan found herself ushered into an airy living room which overlooked the valley.

'You have marvellous views,' she enthused; she was, unusually, at a loss for words.

'It makes up for some of the inconveniences of living out here. Sit down, Rowan. You don't mind me calling you that? We are related in an odd kind of way.' She laughed nervously and twisted her hands together. Rowan winced. 'You must, of course, call me Laura. I'd like that. I'd like it very much. Please do sit down.' Rowan did so, not altogether eagerly. 'Would you like tea?'

Rowan found her voice again. 'No, thank you, Mrs Kingsley. I had a lager at The Duck and Gun before I came here.' She looked up at the woman and added pointedly, 'I came for the jewellery my mother left me.'

Laura Kingsley searched Rowan's face, which was a slightly unnerving experience. The woman backed away from her, towards the door. 'Yes, of course you have. I'll get it. I won't be a moment.'

Rowan drew a small sigh. She'd been rude while Laura Kingsley in her awkward fashion had only tried to be friendly. The events of twenty years ago had been no more Mrs Kingsley's fault than her own.

She gazed around, comparing the shabby comfort of this room, with its faded brocade sofas and worn floor-coverings, to the elegance of her father's palatial apartment furnished with antiques and rare carpets.

Rowan went over to the window again, unable to resist the view. At some time the small panes had been removed and a modern picture window had replaced them to make the most of the view across the valley.

She was standing there still, gazing down at the hill slope and the conifers that marched down to the tarn, when Laura Kingsley returned. For a woman seemingly without much grace she walked surprisingly lightly. Rowan smiled at her in an attempt to make amends for her previous brusqueness; she didn't want this woman to think her mercenary; that she had come only to collect the jewellery. That had only been an excuse to call.

When the older woman sat down on one of the sofas, she motioned for Rowan to join her. Rowan opened the box she was given and took out the gold locket.

'Open it,' Laura urged, and Rowan did so. Inside she found a photograph of a small child; a child with golden curls.

'Why, it's me,' she murmured.

'Yes, and the other photograph is of me and my brothers. You can remove it, of course, if you wish. It's quite a simple matter.'

Rowan drew her gaze from her own photograph to the one facing it. It was of three young people; a boy of about five, an older boy, and Laura in her middle teens.

She closed the locket carefully. 'I wouldn't dream of removing it,' she said to her own surprise. 'I shall keep it as she wore it.'

Brusquely, Laura Kingsley said, 'There's her engagement ring here, too. It's the one your father bought her. It's very valuable, but it meant nothing to us, so she decided to leave it to you. The other things belonged to her before she married my father.'

The ring flashed in Rowan's palm. Two large diamonds flanked a superb emerald. The other item was also in the box. An amethyst mounted in a filagree setting dangled on a fine gold chain.

There was little Rowan could find to say as she replaced them all carefully in the box and closed the lid. She was strangely moved, but she couldn't say why.

'Have you any photographs of her?' she asked. 'I don't even know what she looked like.'

The older woman jumped to her feet. 'Why, yes, yes, of course I have.' She went across the room and came back with a silver-framed photograph. 'This was taken just after they got married. I'm afraid I haven't anything more recent, but we've never bothered too much about photographs. I don't know why. I believe it's all the craze nowadays to take photographs all the time.'

Rowan glanced at it. The man was dark and attractive in a quiet sort of way; the woman could have been found in any crowd. There was little in her features to distinguish her. She tried hard to find some resemblance to herself, but failed, and handed the photograph back without comment.

Laura Kingsley was looking at her. When Rowan met her eyes she was surprised at the hardness she saw there. 'Does he know you're here?'

'My father, you mean?'

'Yes.'

Rowan was forced to look away. 'No, he doesn't.'

A hissing sound escaped Laura Kingsley's lips. 'It was as I expected. If he knew he wouldn't have let you come. That was why I didn't really expect to see you.'

Rowan's head snapped up and her eyes flashed with fire. 'Mrs Kingsley, my father has never forbidden me to do anything. He has always respected my independence and if he knew about my trip here he'd have respected my decision to come.'

It was Laura Kingsley's turn to look away. 'Forgive me, I hadn't meant to . . . speak so harshly.'

'There's no point in not mentioning it. My mother, it seems, left me and my father so that she could marry someone else. Isn't that so? Why be delicate about it?'

'I'm sure you're entitled to be bitter too, Rowan. He must have filled you with a great deal of poison against her.'

Rowan's eyes grew wider. 'He certainly did not! I didn't even know she existed until I got that letter from the solicitor. I'd always believed my mother died when I was three years old.'

'So that's how it was done,' the woman said softly. 'He certainly didn't invite awkward questions, did he?' She looked at Rowan doubtfully. 'But surely he must have spoken of her at some time.'

'Very little. He's not a sentimental man and as I never knew her I wasn't very curious. I once asked to see the grave — she was supposed to have died in Scotland — but for some reason I never went.'

'It was in Scotland that she met my father.'

Rowan got to her feet. 'I must go, Mrs Kingsley. I've detained you far too long already. I appreciate your letting me come. I'm very grateful to you.'

Laura Kingsley looked astounded. 'You can't go just like that. You're not going straight back to London right now, are you?'

Rowan kept her face averted. 'I intended to spend a few days in this part of the country before I go back. I think this has all been more of a shock than I realised at first, so a few days away from everyone will do me good. The landlord at The Duck and Gun says there is a room free tonight.'

'You can't stay there! We have lots of room here — too much room now. Whatever will people think if we let you stay at the inn? No, you must stay here with us. You can use the house as an hotel if you wish. Every part of the Lake District can easily be reached from here.'

'No . . . no, really,' Rowan answered quickly. She wanted nothing more than to leave now. 'I couldn't.'

Laura Kingsley got to her feet. She caught Rowan's arm. 'Oh, please do. I do so want you to stay. Obviously my letter wasn't clear enough; I didn't merely want you to come just for the jewellery. I wanted you to stay for a while. Besides, you haven't met my brothers or my husband. They'll be so disappointed if they miss you, and they'll be angry with me for not making you stay.'

It seemed a sincere request. In fact, Laura Kingsley radiated sincerity, although she suspected her offer of hospitality was due to a feeling of guilt at Delia Halstead's twenty-year-old aberration.

Against her better judgement, Rowan sat down again. 'I'd hate to cause you trouble . . . '

The older woman beamed. 'It's no trouble. I'm glad to have you. Now Delia is no longer here, it gets rather lonely when the men are out each day. Of course, you may not have known about us, but to us you have been a real person for a very long time.'

'Is Mr Halstead dead, too?' Rowan asked, for the want of something to say. Laura Kingsley's reference to her mother, the first allusion to her as a person, was disconcerting.

'My father died seven years ago.'

Rowan still felt uncomfortable. She didn't want to stay. It was such an odd situation she had become involved in. After a moment or two she forced herself to say, 'I feel dreadful not knowing what happened. Will you tell me?'

All goodwill disappeared from Laura Kingsley's manner. 'I think not, Rowan. The bitterness didn't touch you at all, and it's best it should remain so. That was always Delia's wish.'

'But I shall certainly demand to know the story when I see my father, and he will tell me. If I am to stay, I can hardly remain in total ignorance of what happened.'

'Yes, I suppose you're right,' she answered doubtfully. 'I should tell you. Your father thinks he has his reasons for feeling bitter, no doubt, but I should hate you to go through life resenting her.'

'If I hear both stories, I can judge properly.'

Laura looked at her thoughtfully for a moment or two and it was as if she were assessing her. 'Yes, I believe you would judge dispassionately.

'I remember it all very well. I was

already in my teens when it happened. So was Damon, my elder brother, and he remembers it all too, but Chris was too young to know much about it. Our mother died when Chris was born, which is odd, I always think, because he is the only one of the three of us who looks like her. She was very beautiful and gay. Not at all like me, you'll have noticed.' She gave a nervous little laugh. At that moment Rowan realised Laura Kingsley was as uncomfortable about the matter as she was herself. 'Mother loved parties and hunts, and everything connected with the social scene. My father was fond of more leisurely pleasures.' She smiled. 'I'm rambling again, but it's all relevant.'

'Tell it how you wish . . . Laura. I'm not going anywhere.'

'You are a nice child,' Laura said suddenly. 'I knew you would be even though Da . . . Oh, where was I? Yes, of course. Well, it seems your parents were invited to a country weekend at Lord Rothmere's place in Scotland. It was to be a hunting, shooting and fishing party which your father loves, I believe.' Rowan nodded her agreement.

Laura got up. She went over to the mantelpiece, put the photograph down on it and began to adjust some of the ornaments standing there. 'My mother was dead by then and my father was lonely, I suppose. Anyway, the Rothmeres were more friends of my late mother's than Father, but apparently he felt he should accept their invitation, if only out of politeness. It seems Delia didn't particularly want to go either, so when the others were out she and my father stayed behind. They had long talks; discovered interests in common. That's how it started.'

'When my father went to London on business soon afterwards, he asked her out to lunch.' Laura turned round again. 'You see, it wasn't deliberate wickedness. It just happened. It's something that happens so often and just as innocently, don't you agree?'

Rowan looked down at the box she

still held in her hands. She resented Laura Kingsley's attempts to excuse her mother's behaviour and it was disconcerting that the woman was no longer embarrassed or ill at ease.

'It's easy to be sympathetic when the matter doesn't involve oneself. She was a married woman. She should have known better.'

Laura Kingsley helped herself to a cigarette from a silver box after offering it to Rowan. Rowan shook her head. She could hardly believe the events recounted by this woman could have involved her parents; the mother she had imagined to be dead. If she had never mourned her consciously she had attributed it to the skill with which her father had managed her upbringing.

Laura lit the cigarette with a table lighter that matched the box. She inhaled deeply and gazed at Rowan for a moment; then she flopped down into an easy chair, crossing her thick legs, with her tweed skirt hitched almost to her thighs.

'As you say, it's easy to sympathise from afar, but it's just as easy to condemn. Of course she was a married woman and of course she did wrong. But falling in love with my father wasn't a deliberate act. I'm sure, living the life you do, a modern young woman like yourself, you often eat out with a married friend and think nothing of it. But you could so easily fall in love with a married man without realising it was even happening.'

'If it did happen to me, I hope I — and he — would know where our duty lie.'

'Well,' Laura said with a smile that made Rowan feel both young and prudish, 'I can do no more than tell it how it happened and you must judge it as you will. Unless, of course, you've already heard enough. Believe me, Rowan, I'm trying to be as unbiased as I can, but it's very difficult. She was in every way a wonderful mother to me.'

Rowan looked up quickly, trying not to be hurt by Laura's last remark.

Heaven knew, with all her father's friends and acquaintances around her for the past twenty years, she had grown up with a broad outlook on life.

'This is rather embarrassing,' she admitted. 'One somehow expects one's parents to be above that kind of thing.'

Laura laughed, wryly, as she knocked off a column of ash from her cigarette. 'How true.' And how Rowan wished she, too, had twenty years' familiarity with those events. 'Damon and I were in our teens, as I've already explained, when it happened and there isn't a more self-conscious age, and I can tell you quite truthfully there was quite a lot to be self-conscious about.

'I know you might find this difficult to understand, but she was dreadfully unhappy before she met my father. Please let me go on,' she begged as Rowan was about to speak. 'It isn't easy to talk about it even now, so I'd like to finish and we can talk about more pleasant matters.

'She *was* unhappy, Rowan. Oh, it's

true your father was a good husband. His wife had furs and jewellery and a beautiful home. But she needed more than that; she needed her husband with her. He was away very often on business and when he wasn't away he was taking her to house parties. They were hardly ever alone together. Delia was quite a shy person — quite the wrong wife for a man like Louis Patrick, although she loved him very much at first.

'Eventually she knew she couldn't continue to be married to him. She wanted nothing of a squalid affair; she wanted to marry my father, and it wasn't an easy decision for her to make.'

'And?' Rowan asked, knowing the unpleasant part must come next.

Laura crushed out the cigarette that was burning down between her fingers. 'She asked for a divorce.' She took a deep breath. 'The fury of a woman scorned had nothing on the fury of your father.'

Rowan had seen her father in a temper and it was never a pleasant sight. 'I'd say they deserved his fury.'

'Perhaps, but he could have given in with more grace. Anger soon dies. Your father, forgive me, Rowan, was not an innocent. Before then and since, I believe, he has been very attractive to women. Your mother would have been quite satisfied to be the 'guilty' party if the divorce could have been arranged quietly, but he was determined to be as unpleasant as possible and to revenge himself by claiming sole custody of you, so she had to fight.'

'And she lost.'

'Yes, she lost,' Laura answered with a sigh. 'It was in all the newspapers. Your father was a prominent figure even then. It was one of those social scandals that people revel in. In those days divorce wasn't the easy matter it is today, or nearly as acceptable. It was a dreadful time for us all. It took her a long time to live down her bad reputation, but she managed it eventually; people came to respect her as she deserved and we lived very happily.'

'I can't understand why she didn't try to see me, to explain herself — later, when I was older and able to understand and judge for myself.'

'Because she knew it would revive all the old bitterness and hatred and she didn't want you to be involved. She knew you'd be well cared for. He adored you and could give you anything you wanted. She reckoned that even if she'd remained married to him you would have grown up strange to her. He insisted that you have a nanny and with them being away so much she saw little of you. She didn't want him to use you as a weapon against her, with you suffering the most. She could have fought for years over the custody order; my father consulted several barristers on the matter. But, as I said, Delia was afraid of what prolonged litigation would do to you.

'Oh, yes, she did try to see you on one occasion. It was a couple of years later. Father was going to London on business and she accompanied him. She went round to where you were living and just waited outside until you were brought out. It upset her so much that she refused to go to London again, and she never did.'

'Did she never have any more children?' Rowan asked.

It was all so different to how she had imagined it to be. She didn't doubt her father's actions as recounted by Laura; Rowan knew him too well. He was a hard man, a passionate man, who would not let go easily. She didn't blame him his fury; she could understand it well enough, only she wished he had acted more compassionately, both for her own sake and for the sake of the mother she would never now know.

'No,' Laura answered, 'and I think it was quite deliberate that she didn't. We were all growing up and we'd had quite a battering from the gossip and publicity. I really believe she decided to devote herself to making us a happy family. The divorce didn't end the unpleasantness.'

Rowan looked at her expectantly and Laura's lips twisted into a bitter smile. 'She told me about it years later, after I was married myself. When they were leaving the court he threatened them. He hadn't caused us enough misery, it seemed.

'We have a manufacturing company — drugs and chemicals. Your father has contacts in every industry and he promised to use them to ruin our business. He wasn't satisfied with having deprived her of her child and humiliating us all publicly; to use his own words, he was going to reduce us to penury, and he certainly did try. Luckily we've been manufacturing for many years — my grandfather started the company — and our name is good. What little business we lost was soon made up and eventually Patrick gave up trying and we were left in peace.'

Rowan recalled her father boasting

on frequent occasions of his business successes and made no secret of the methods used, but she had always believed it to be usual business practice. It seemed incredible to believe that he would embark upon a vendetta as vicious as this one for purely personal reasons.

'I hardly know what to say. I'm so sorry.'

'My dear child, there is no need for you to be sorry. You were hardly more than a baby at the time. He was wrong to do what he did, and he was wrong to pretend your mother was dead. But he obviously felt himself deeply wronged and I think it's to his credit that he has never slandered her to you. We often wondered what he would tell you when you were old enough to ask.'

She looked at Rowan anxiously. 'You will stay, won't you, dear? Chris and my husband will be in for dinner, but Damon is out tonight. You'll see him tomorrow though, if you get up early enough, that is,' she added with a laugh.

'I do want you to stay. Say you will.'

Rowan looked around her and then back to the hopeful face of Laura Kingsley. She could hardly refuse to stay now she had heard the full story. 'In the circumstances,' she answered slowly, 'it's good of you to want me here.'

'As I said, no one blames you. We can't pretend not to be bitter at your father still, but that need not concern you.' She got to her feet. 'Come along. I'll show you to your room. Now, just remember you're not to be tied here; treat this house just as you would an hotel . . . '

Rowan glanced behind her as she followed Laura out of the room and gave an almost imperceptible sigh. She had known it all along — it would have been much simpler if she'd collected the jewellery from the solicitor.

3

'Ah, so there you are. Come along in.'

It was about an hour later. Rowan had unpacked her belongings, washed and changed into a simple silk sheath dress. Dinner was still far ahead when she had completed these simple chores, so she had drawn a chair up to the bedroom window that overlooked the tarn and had brooded upon all that Laura Kingsley had told her.

After a while she became weary of thinking of those sad events. It was, unfortunately, not in her power to change them and therefore useless to brood on all the unhappiness that had been caused to both sides, so she went downstairs to seek company.

The voice that invited her into the living room as she had peered hesitantly around the door belonged to a man who was just pouring himself a large whisky from one of the many decanters set out on a tray. Hamish was curled on a sheepskin rug in front of the fireplace. His ears pricked at the sight of her and then his nose subsided into his paws again.

'Would you like a drink?' the man asked. 'A sherry, perhaps?'

'I'll have the same as you, if I may — with soda, please,' she told him as she came right into the room. He wasn't much above average height, slightly stout, with fair hair that was beginning to thin.

As he handed her the glass he studied her face and she started to say, 'I'm . . .'

'Yes, I know who you are. I'm Robert Kingsley. My wife has told me all about you.'

He held out his hand and Rowan found hers taken in his firm grip. 'I know all about Louis Patrick,' he said with a grin. 'Of course, it was all before my time, so I can't get all het up about it. But I must say I'm glad you're here.

I don't believe in feuds.'

'Thanks,' she answered, flushing slightly.

'Laura's delighted to have you here. You'll do her good. Even though she keeps busy with one thing and another, she's been moping since Delia died. They were more like sisters really. I must say I miss her myself.'

He finished off his drink and refilled his glass. Rowan walked over to the window to gaze out on the view. 'You all live together in this house quite happily, don't you?'

Robert Kingsley came over to join her. 'Can you think of a nicer place? I can't. I was brought up in a city.' His voice was suddenly harsh as if he didn't like the memory. 'There's plenty of room here, and Laura's always loved it. I suppose when Damon marries, though, he'll have his own place.'

'So he's engaged,' she said.

'Sort of.' Rowan swung round at the sound of an unfamiliar voice. The young man who had come in was fair-haired. His face was tanned and his body slim and lithe like that of an athlete. His grey eyes lingered on Rowan and she felt that she had been looked at like that before. 'He'll make it official one day — when he finds the time between experiments. Poor Carolyne would get more attention if she were a laboratory mouse or a guinea pig.'

Rowan frowned. Carolyne? The girl who ran the riding stables was Carolyne Griffin. Rowan suddenly remembered the man who had been with that girl and she had a feeling of foreboding.

Robert laughed. 'Come along in, Chris, and meet our guest.'

He looked at her again. 'That is something I have every intention of doing.'

At that moment they were joined by Laura who was now wearing a dress with a floral pattern that did nothing for her shape or colouring.

'Oh,' she said breathlessly when she saw them all together, 'I'm sorry I'm late. Are you getting acquainted?'

'I'm trying to,' complained the young man, 'but no one, so far, has seen fit to make the introduction.'

Laura took his hand. She looked at him and there was a slight anxiety in her tone as she said, 'Chris, this is Rowan Patrick.' She quickly went on to explain the letter and the invitation. Rowan was not happy to hear that Laura had not consulted the other members of her family before writing or issuing the invitation to come to Skelvingsdale.

'You are a dark horse, Laura,' Chris said with a laugh, and Rowan was relieved to find no resentment in his manner towards her, 'but a clever one. I'd never have thought of it myself.' He went up to Rowan then and took her hand in his. 'So this is little Rowan. Welcome to Skelvingsdale.'

Rowan withdrew her hand rather self-consciously. 'Thank you. I'm glad I came.'

'Let's go in to dinner, shall we?'

Laura urged, and her tone plainly suggested relief. 'Afterwards we can all get to know Rowan better. She's staying with us for a few days. Isn't that nice?'

* * *

The oak refectory table seemed enormous with only four people present. Rowan sat back in her chair as the others talked to her and amongst themselves of various topics — all of them neutral. The reason for this was the presence of Mrs Jennings and Mary, who served the meal. Rowan knew that Chris Halstead cast her frequent speculative glances and had done so continually throughout dinner. He admired her, she knew, and he was attractive enough for her to enjoy his admiration. He caught her eye across the table and she smiled at him.

She wondered what her father would say if he knew she was in this house. There would be angry words exchanged over it, this she would have to face, but relaxed at last in the midst of such goodwill as had been shown towards her, she was not sorry she had come.

'You'll be needing a guide to show you around,' said Chris as he finished off the last of his wine. 'You won't know your way around.'

'I can read a map quite well,' she told him, smiling again.

'The best places aren't shown on the map.'

'Chris won't be put off easily,' Robert told her. 'He can be very persistent to get something he wants.'

Chris laughed. 'You've been warned, Rowan.'

'But what about your work, Chris?'

He laughed again. 'I'm what would once have been called the ne'er-do-well. Laura does good work in the neighbourhood and Damon keeps the factory going by working twenty hours in every twenty-four. I do nothing and love every minute of it.'

'It's true,' Laura put in when she saw Rowan's disbelief. She seemed not at all put out by her brother's admission, no more than she was about his constant cynicism, which led Rowan to believe, as it so often did, that it masked a real affection for his family.

'When my father died,' Laura went on to explain, 'he divided his share of the business equally between us all. My share, of course, went to Robert — he's the company secretary — and Chris sold his to Damon. The Halstead holding has always been the main one, and when Chris sold his to Damon it made his position even stronger. He needs a strong position to be able to keep on with his research. It's very costly.'

'And it gave me enough money to enable me to spend my days at leisure.'

'Don't forget your interest in Carolyne's stables,' his sister pointed out.

'Oh, I'm not likely to do that.' A strange smile twisted his lips. He turned to Rowan again. 'When I was paid out for the shares, I sunk some of the money into the riding stables. Carolyne and I have a very good business arrangement. It gives me something to do now and again. Carolyne loves horses but hates bookwork, so I take care of that for her. It doesn't demand too much of my time — I get a small return for my investment — and that's what makes it particularly attractive to me.'

'I shouldn't think a riding school is a very lucrative venture for you to sink your money into,' Rowan ventured.

Chris shrugged. 'It's sufficient to occupy a rich man's daughter until she marries, and it will do for me until I marry a rich wife. That's what I'm really after. It's a trait that runs in our family; I should hate to be the odd one out.'

Rowan was puzzled until she saw a flush creep up Robert Kingsley's cheeks. And then Laura said quickly, 'Let's go into the living room for our coffee. It's cosier there.'

The conversation was desultory, slightly embarrassed until Mrs Jennings had left the tray. The housekeeper, Rowan found, had given her covert looks during the meal and from the way her lips tightened together as she did so, Rowan guessed that the woman did not approve of her presence.

Laura poured and handed round the coffee. Rowan stirred hers thoughtfully. 'Did you know that some of the people in the area believe your factory is a germ-warfare establishment?'

Laura and Robert laughed as one, and Chris looked annoyed. 'Blame Damon for that. He sees himself as some super James Bond.' Rowan looked at him and he said in a mock whisper, 'Industrial espionage. More deadly than the international kind. Spies can be lurking behind every filing cabinet and every desk. They even employ a retired flatfoot as a full-time security officer.'

Rowan laughed, too, at the way he spoke and Laura added, in a good-humoured way, 'There isn't one person who doesn't know what is really going on at our factory. But that's too mundane to give the gossips something to talk about. They prefer to suggest something far more sinister.'

'What exactly *is* being done?' Rowan asked.

'Research into new drugs, improvements to old ones. There are quite a number of our competitors who would love to have an inkling as to what is being done.'

'At the moment,' Robert added, packing his pipe in a thoughtful way, 'Damon is pursuing a pet project of his which could turn out to be pretty important. Chris may well joke about it, but our precautions are very necessary.'

'There doesn't seem much point to me,' Chris answered lazily. He took his coffee cup and went across to the window. 'If anyone wants to know anything at all, bribing one of the staff with a few pounds would do the job just as well as a full-scale break-in, which is all the security guards are preventing. If industrial espionage is such a serious problem, it's the work of experts, not common burglars.'

'That's why all the staff are carefully vetted,' Robert told him, drawing ineffectually at his pipe. He shook his head and attempted to relight it again.

'Your brother is in charge of the research, I believe?' Rowan asked politely, addressing Laura, who was more likely to give a straight answer.

'Yes, that's right. We're keeping it right in the family. My father was quite content to pack and sell just as our grandfather did, and Jim Griffin was quite happy to go along with that. No company should stagnate in that way. The firm needed someone new so that it could expand and grow stronger. My brother is just what was needed. He was responsible for building the new laboratories. It's to be hoped it pays off eventually. He's very highly qualified.'

Chris turned round. 'The door to his office has an extra-wide door — so that there's enough room to paint on all the letters after his name.'

'Oh, really, Chris,' Laura laughed.

'It's true. And he's very single-minded. He decided when he was still a schoolboy that the firm needed someone with high scientific qualifications and went on to get them. He believes anything he really wants to do is possible. It's a good philosophy when one comes to think about it. I wish I could be like that, too. I've always believed that Damon could become a lead dancer with the Bolshoi Ballet if he put his mind to it.'

'Doesn't he sound awful?' Laura said, laughingly, to Rowan, 'but he's always like this. Nothing and no one is sacred.' She glanced at him and there was no mistaking the fondness her look held. 'Why don't you take Rowan out for a walk, Chris? It's a lovely evening.'

He came across to Rowan's chair and put his hands on the back of it, looking down at her. 'I was just going to suggest it. I've been polite for long enough. Now I'm going to have her to myself for a while. Come along. Hamish, you can chaperon.'

*　*　*

When Rowan went to her room to fetch a cardigan she doubted the wisdom of going out with Chris Halstead. He was an odd man — strangely attractive — and she found him hard to understand. But it was a truly lovely evening and after her conversation with Laura Kingsley earlier, she badly needed the fresh air.

'I want to show you something interesting,' Chris told her when they were outside. Hamish padded obediently ahead of them.

Behind the house the garden had been terraced up the slope of the hill. Not far from the house a beck ran down the side of the hill and where it passed closest to the house a rock garden, ablaze with colour, had been built around the water.

'She built this herself,' Chris said as Rowan let out a little gasp of pleasure, 'with only Laura to help. She was very good with her hands. Her flower arrangements were quite remarkable.'

Rowan smiled grimly to herself. Her father had often wondered how she came by her artistic talent, for he had none; but he had known all the time.

'Do you ride?' he asked abruptly as if he sensed the uncomfortable train of her thoughts.

'I did, but I haven't done any for years.'

'Perhaps you'll find the time while you're here. I'll take you down and fix you up with a mount. It's good riding country.'

'I think I'd like to renew my acquaintance with our four-legged friends. I used to enjoy riding. My father always hoped I would ride to hounds with him, but I don't like hunting.'

'Neither do we, but we are the exception. There's a great deal of hunting in the autumn. Devotees will tell you that it's necessary to keep the foxes down, and I don't doubt it's true, but I'd as soon shoot the poor devils and be done with it. Jim Griffin's the master of the Harvington Hunt. The whole family join in. It's quite a sight to see Belinda Griffin — she's Carolyne's mother — in full cry. She's sixteen stone and has a voice like a sergeant-major.

'Shall we follow the beck?' he invited a few moments later after she had admired the rock garden at closer quarters.

Rowan inhaled the fresh evening air. The clouds had cleared and hardly a breeze stirred the leaves. 'Where does it lead to?'

'The tarn down there. There are over four hundred of them in the district, of varying sizes. Some are no more than pools.'

'I've never been here before, but I wish I had,' she told him as they wandered along by the side of the beck.

He smiled. 'You've been kept away from this part of the world quite skilfully.'

'It looks like it.' She looked at him.

'Laura told me all about it this afternoon, Chris, and my father didn't come out of it very well. Was there any chance that she was exaggerating?'

Chris gave a harsh laugh. 'Laura? She wouldn't know how to exaggerate,' he added, confirming Rowan's own opinion of Laura Kingsley.

He stopped walking. They were half-way down the hill. Hamish had reached the bottom and was frisking happily amongst the green fronds of new bracken. The clouds had dispersed and the evening sun was flaming the sky. It had turned the grey slab of water into something that looked like a pool of blood.

Rowan shivered. 'Delia was the only mother I ever knew, and as far back as I can remember she was there. She always seemed perfectly happy and contented with us. When I grew up I was told all about it, but I can't remember any unpleasantness, so I have no personal grudge against him. But as far as I can see, Louis Patrick is a number one rat.'

Rowan winced again. He put his hand on her arm. 'You asked me and it's not in my nature to prevaricate, Rowan. No one is going to hold it against you. Everyone has their detractors, your father being as he is, more than most, but it doesn't affect your relationship with him, or with anyone else.' He squeezed her arm briefly. 'Come on, let's walk. There's a good view of the house from down there. The climb back will get you good and tired. You'll sleep like the dead tonight.'

It seemed that with Chris Halstead it was impossible to remain serious for long.

'Why did you make that remark about members of your family marrying for money?' she asked as she hurried to keep up with his long-legged stride.

'I have a sense of humour no one appreciates. Robert hasn't got a sense of humour at all. When Laura met him he was studying accountancy and having a rough time of it. The family was poor, very poor, and he wasn't bringing in any money. They were urging him to get a job in a factory where he could earn a great deal of money straight away; it was the only thing they understood. Then he met Laura and his problems were solved. Now he has a big, fat shareholding in a go-ahead firm like Halstead and Griffin.'

'That doesn't mean he married Laura just for her money.'

'Perhaps not, but that little joke hits a bit too close to home for Robert's comfort.' He glanced at Rowan. 'And then there's Damon. One of these days he's going to look up from his microscope and decide it's time to make an honest woman of Carolyne, and as she is Jim Griffin's only daughter it won't do Damon's position in the company any harm at all. It will mean that eventually he'll have complete control of the firm.'

Rowan shook her head and laughed. 'What a cynic you are!'

They had reached the flat ground surrounding the water. 'Perhaps I am. Now I'm looking forward to discovering what *you* are, Rowan.'

Deliberately she drew her eyes away from his and gazed around her at the purple splendour of the fells and crags surrounding them. Skelvingsdale Hall soared above them amidst the trees and Rowan said, 'You were right, Chris, it's a marvellous view of the house. It looks just like an eagle lording it over the valley. I should love to paint it just as it looks from here.'

He looked at her in amazement. 'You paint?'

'Not as much as I'd like to for pleasure. I'm a commercial artist, but one day I've promised myself time to paint for pleasure and I've a good mind to start right now. I can paint a picture of the house and if it isn't too bad I can give it to Laura before I go.'

'She'd like that.' He studied her carefully for a moment. She was aware of it, although she pretended to be admiring the scenery. 'So you are staying?'

The tone of his voice made it difficult for her to look at him again. She liked him. She felt that he could be a pleasant and an amusing companion, but an inner sense told her that, attractive as he was, there could be nothing more.

'For a little while, anyway.'

'How about staying until after next Friday?'

'Next Friday? Why, what is happening next Friday?'

The cynical smile returned to his lips. 'Halstead and Griffin are having their midsummer dinner and dance at Harvington Golf Club next Friday. There'll be a jolly good meal, plenty to drink, and Jim Griffin will stand up and make the same speech he's made for every year past, trotting out all the usual cliches about noses to the grindstone and backs to the wall and winning through in the end. I can repeat it to you word for word now. No one listens. We all shuffle our feet underneath the table until he finishes and we can go and dance.'

She laughed as he went on, 'I wasn't planning to go this year although I should, but if you'd go with me I'd have an incentive, and to see you there would give a lot of people a thrill; something new for them to talk about.'

'I'm not sure I want to be talked about,' she said carefully.

'You're obviously not used to places like Skelvingsdale.' She looked at him quizzically. 'You stopped at The Duck and Gun on the way here,' he explained patiently. 'Without a doubt, you're being talked about already and if you decide not to stay, it will be said that we chased you away. But that's not my reason for wanting you here. You know that, don't you?'

'Chris, I think I should tell you that I am getting engaged when I go back to London.'

His eyes looked into hers steadily.

'That makes no difference. I'm surprised that you think it should. You've just learned that my father walked off with another man's wife.' Her gaze did not waver from his, and he added, 'Well, now you've told me. But he's in London and you are here, and you're not engaged yet. Who is he, anyway? A young tycoon, perhaps?'

'He's an architect; rather a good one, too.'

Chris smiled. 'It seems that I'm always being out-classed by the bright boys.'

The breeze was coming up again and it was growing cool. She wondered for the first time if Chris Halstead had been disappointed over Carolyne Griffin. If he had, she felt he would not show it in an obvious way. A quick grin, an acid comment, was the way he would cover up his hurt.

'Do you resent your brother? I have the feeling that you do, although I'm sure you could succeed in anything you set your mind on, too.'

'Do you indeed? No, I don't resent Damon. He and I are as different as can be, and it enables us to like and respect each other much more than if we were both of the same mind. Shall we go back? You look cold and it will almost be dark by the time we get to the house.'

They started back, the hill being steeper than Rowan had realised on the walk down. Chris looked at her sideways. 'And does Daddy approve of your bright young architect? Not much of a match for Louis Patrick's daughter, I should have thought.'

'Whatever you think, my father approves.'

'Would you still marry him if he didn't approve?'

Chris was back to his maddeningly cynical mood, and Rowan answered coldly, 'The question doesn't arise.'

'But if it did, would you persist?'

'How could I possibly know?'

'If your father disapproved of the man you intended to marry, he'd probably go all out to destroy him, and now, more than twenty years ago, he has the means to do it. You might end up living in poverty in an attic in some damp, rat-infested slum.'

Rowan laughed, but it was a harsh sound. 'I doubt it. You really have a vivid imagination. There are few enough men my father would dislike so much, and I doubt if I would consider marrying any of them.'

'He hoped to ruin my father, but he didn't succeed.'

'He can't have tried hard enough.' She looked at him as she paused to rest, breathless now. 'Doesn't anyone ever call you Christopher?'

He laughed, and his laugh echoed around the crags and the quiet valley. 'Never. That isn't my name. It's Christian. Now there's something of a contradiction. If anyone called me by my full name I think they would feel as though they were blaspheming.'

The collie had reached the wide ledge on which the house had been built, and was running to and fro, barking his encouragement. Chris took her hand and began to pull her along the path back to the house, and when they reached it they were still laughing.

4

As Chris predicted, Rowan slept well that night. She awoke the following morning to a sharp knocking at her door.

'Get up, lazybones!' came Chris Halstead's unmistakable voice. 'We're going out!'

'Give me fifteen minutes,' she replied, and then curled back under the covers.

She lay there for some time longer, between sleep and waking. Through the heavy haze of half-sleep she could hear the tread of a man's footsteps passing her door at intervals. The whole house seemed alive, but Rowan had no desire to rush. It was a full year since her last holiday, and between then and now she had worked unbelievably hard to build up a reputation as an artist. There had been many parties, too, especially since she'd met Tony, and very few early nights.

It seemed incredible that a week ago she hadn't known these people existed and now they could so easily become an important part of her life. Despite everything that had happened, there was still a link . . .

When she came down the stairs she found Chris in the hall peering at the mail. Mary, the maid, was doing her best to attract his attention as she fluttered around the hall, dusting this and adjusting that.

'Sorry I kept you waiting,' she apologised.

'There's the rest of the day,' he answered with a smile, and then, to Mary with an equally charming smile which flustered the girl, 'We're ready for our breakfast now, Mary.'

'Something tells me you play havoc with the emotions of the domestic staff,' Rowan said in a low voice as Mary hurried off towards the kitchen. His answering laugh proved quite plainly that he was well aware of that fact.

He took her arm and led her into the small breakfast room which, unlike the dining room, overlooked the valley. 'This is a nice place to start the day,' she murmured as they took their places at the table. 'It would soothe the grumpiest disposition.'

'Sometimes it needs to.' A moment later he said, 'Laura's gone out. She planned to visit some friends for the day and when I assured her that you'd be well looked after in her absence, she decided not to cancel the arrangements. I hope you approve.'

'Oh, certainly. I'd have hated her to have cancelled any plans for my sake. I don't want to be any trouble to anyone while I'm here.'

'You'll be no trouble to me,' he answered, giving her one of his ready grins.

Soon after breakfast they set off in her car — his had been sold recently and he was awaiting a new one — and as the solid grey clouds overhead augured rain Chris suggested that they postpone their trip to the lakes.

'Let's go to Kendal,' Rowan suggested, 'and I can buy my paints there.'

She soon found a shop that sold all that she needed, and as she came out she glanced idly in the window of the dress shop next door. On an impulse she bundled all the parcels into Chris's arms, saying, 'Take these back to the car, Chris, and meet me back here in about half an hour from now. I've just seen a dress I fancy.'

He laughed and shook his head. 'I should have known better than to come shopping with a woman.'

The dress she had spotted in the window was a long evening dress of scarlet-and-white chiffon. Scarlet doesn't always suit girls with hair as fair as Rowan's, but her skin was dark, as were her eyes. It was a striking combination, although she wasn't fully aware the effect it often had on the opposite sex.

Providentially, the dress was her size and needed no alteration. Rowan didn't need to hear the assistant effusively commending the dress and the way she looked in it; Rowan could see for herself how its soft folds swirled and clung around her figure, and she promptly wrote out a cheque for the amount asked. As she did so she recalled, wryly, the number of evening dresses that were hanging in the big wardrobes in her father's apartment. She had come north with the bare minimum of clothes; an evening dress was the last garment she would have thought of bringing along.

Rowan left the shop well pleased with her purchases — she had also suc-cumbed to the charms of a day dress and bought that, too. Up until now she hadn't quite made up her mind to accept Chris's invitation to the dance, but Friday was only a few days away, and, in a typically female fashion, the dress had finally settled the matter.

When she came out of the dress shop with the carefully wrapped dresses in her arms, she peered anxiously up and down the street; Chris was nowhere to be seen. She glanced at her watch and found that she had spent five minutes over the half-hour in the shop, but she couldn't pretend to be surprised; even without knowing him well, Chris Halstead was not a man she would have considered to be punctual.

She considered going back to the car, but realised that if she did she would probably miss him completely, so she resigned herself to wait, trying to look as inconspicuous as possible.

She had been waiting only a minute or two when she sensed that someone was looking at her. Instinctively she glanced across the road. With something of a shock her eyes met those of the man she had seen outside The Duck and Gun the day before. He hesitated to stare at her for no more than a moment, but as on the previous occasion it seemed so much longer. It was over in a second and then he was gone, around the corner and out of her sight. She felt shaken and when, just then, she saw Chris striding towards her, she hurried up to him, saying breathlessly, 'Oh, I am glad to see you!' with far more warmth than she had intended.

'Well, this is a nice greeting; I take it that you found what you wanted. What a remarkable difference a new dress makes to any woman.'

He took the parcels from her and then her arm to guide her along the street when she made no move to walk herself. Instinctively, she glanced behind her again, along the street into which the man had disappeared.

'I thought you'd be furious with me for being late. Most women would be in a terrible temper at being kept waiting, although they think nothing of keeping a fellow hanging around while they comb their hair or powder their noses.'

'You sound as if you're fully experienced in the ways of women,' she said, finding her voice at last. His gay prattle at least had covered the confusion she was feeling, giving her time to recover.

'What man isn't? A man worth

having, I mean. Even my brother appreciates a comely female, although he would never admit it. Of course, as I've said before, he's not like me!'

'You could at least tell me *why* you kept me waiting.'

'Oh, that. I saw a nice car in a showroom and let them talk me into trying it out.'

'And are you buying it?'

'I'd love to, but it's a wee bit too expensive, unfortunately. My tastes always run higher than my income.'

'You could always work,' she suggested.

'Heaven forbid!' They paused at the edge of the kerb. 'Let's get out of this place. I've had enough of shopping for today. It's always a mistake to let a female loose near shops.'

'I'm your guest, Chris,' she said gaily, 'by all means lead the way.'

★ ★ ★

It was late in the afternoon when they returned to Skelvingsdale. Despite the profusion of grey cloud that had adorned the sky all day, it had not rained and they'd had their lunch at an hotel overlooking Windermere. After that they had walked a little way along the lake shore and then driven into the surrounding countryside. They'd passed countless lakes and tarns, climbed hills and plunged into dales asparkle with streams.

'I've certainly had a Cook's tour today,' she said as they neared the village.

'You've not seen a fraction of it, Rowan.'

'I've seen possibly all that I'm going to see this trip.' He glanced at her. 'This time next week I shall be home.'

'With lover boy.'

'With Tony.'

'Fair enough, but there's time until then. A girl like you shouldn't be tied down to one man.'

'I want only one man. When he's the right one it's all any girl needs.'

A warm glow spread through her

veins at the very thought of it. She had a wonderful future to contemplate. She had always wanted her own home in the country, a man to love her, and children to play on the lawn. It came as a surprise for her to realise how badly she wanted it all. Despite a thriving career, a successful social life and everything money could buy for her comfort, it was almost a primitive urge she felt just then.

'Are you sure he's the right one?' Chris's bantering voice jarred into her lovely thoughts.

'Of course!' she cried, laughing at so ludicrous a question.

He shrugged slightly. 'It was a faint hope. I had a silly idea you've enjoyed my company.'

'And so I have, but I don't love you.'

'We could have fun together.'

'Certainly, whilst I'm here. For longer, I need more than just fun.'

'Daddy has fun.' Rowan looked at him sharply, but his eyes, full of mischief, were on the road.

'My father is entitled to his fun,' she answered drily. 'His one attempt at marriage wasn't all that successful, but he *did* try it first.'

'With your money, Rowan, and my charm we could have lots of fun. Old age comes soon enough.'

'Yes, and when it comes I want someone to share it with.'

'That's a long way off. Too far away for it to bother you.'

'It seems to be bothering you,' she retorted, eyeing him with amusement. She had met his kind before; he would still be struggling to remain a fun-loving playboy if he lived to be eighty years old.

'Why not give it a try? You don't seem to be missing lover boy.'

It was true, Rowan realised, and she felt a pang of guilt. She had hardly thought of Tony for three days and, as it was the first time she had been apart from him for such a long period since they met, Rowan felt that she should be.

'We could shack up together for a while and if things work out, well . . . '

She sat back so that she could study his face better. 'You're not serious?'

When he looked at her there was no laughter in his eyes. 'Don't you think I could fancy you, Rowan? You're very attractive, you know.'

She threw back her head and laughed, which had the effect of disconcerting him. She knew he would have enjoyed her indignation and outrage, but her laughter did not suit him at all.

'Chris! You're priceless. Really marvellous! I've never met anyone quite like you before. Your approach needs attending to. You come to the point far too quickly and much too bluntly for any girl. Haven't you heard of the art of seduction? You practise that first and then make your . . . suggestion.' She laughed again and was relieved when his astonishment turned to amusement, too. 'I don't suppose it's even entered your mind that I might not 'fancy' *you*.'

He grinned. 'As a matter of fact, it hasn't. Should it have done?'

She laughed even more at that. 'See those trees over there?' he said a moment later, and as she looked at the mountain ashes with their feathery fronds she knew what he was going to say next. She recalled that her botany teacher at school took a delight in mentioning it every time they had a nature ramble.

'They're rowans — your namesakes. You should really have red hair to match the berries, so the name doesn't exactly fit you. It makes no difference though, I knew a girl called Virginia once . . . '

'All right, Chris!' she laughed. 'I don't want to hear.'

When they arrived at Skelvingsdale Hall he put his hand on hers to stop her getting out immediately. 'I hope you didn't take offence over what I was saying just now.'

She smiled. 'Even if I took you seriously I wouldn't have taken offence, Chris.'

He released her hand. 'Good. I'd hate you to pack your bags in a fever of virtuous indignation, leaving me to explain to Laura. She'd never understand. And I've got until Friday to make you change your mind.'

'I'll take the dresses,' she told him quickly. 'You bring in the other parcels, please.'

★   ★   ★

The house was quiet when they arrived back. Laura was already changed, and after asking if they'd had a nice day assured Rowan that she had lots of time in which to take a bath.

When she came down she was wearing one of the dresses she had bought that day. She made straight for the sitting room where it was customary for the family to assemble for drinks before dinner. Rowan was already becoming familiar with the family's routine, and it suddenly occurred to her that with all her material advantages and the affection her father unashamedly showered upon her, she had never enjoyed a real family atmosphere at home.

As she crossed the hall she could hear voices in the sitting room and she was glad; she hated being the first down. This was not her home and she still could not feel entirely at ease here.

She was about to push open the door, which was ajar, when an angry voice from within stayed her hand. It began to tremble at the fury she could hear in the unfamiliar voice.

'How long has she been here?'

'Since yesterday.' It was Laura's soft voice that answered.

'Twenty-four hours, and I have to hear it from Josh Naylor at The Duck and Gun!'

'I'm sorry about that, Damon, but you were out yesterday and you must recall that you went out before I was up this morning. I haven't had one chance to tell you.'

Rowan bit her lip. She had no doubt

that it was herself who was the subject of this heated discussion.

'It might have been more reasonable if you'd consuilted the rest of us before you ever wrote that letter, Laura.'

'It never occurred to me.'

'But it should have done. I live here, too.'

'Really, dear? One would hardly realise it these days. Besides, Robert and Chris are quite pleased that she's here.'

'Then they're as short-sighted as you are. Whatever put such a crazy notion into your head, Laura?'

'Because we have a lot in common — Delia. She's her daughter, and I thought enough time had passed . . . Oh, Damon, dear, she's a very nice girl. It's not her fault . . . '

Rowan had the feeling that Damon Halstead was prowling round the room, for his voice was sometimes nearer to her than at other times.

'A nice girl,' he scoffed. 'When will you learn that there are quite a number of people in this world who are *not* nice?'

'You haven't even met her. Why judge her so harshly? She was Delia's daughter, too.'

'She was born to Delia,' he corrected, 'but she was brought up under that man's influence, and I don't have to tell you what that means. If she's only a part like Louis Patrick, its' more than enough.'

Rowan sank back against the wall, pressing her hand to her lips to stifle a cry. There had been so much hatred in his voice; he sounded unbelievably bitter.

'Get rid of her. Make some excuse — any excuse, but see that she leaves here immediately.'

'No, Damon. I've invited her to stay for a few days; I can't suddenly ask her to go for such a silly reason. And I hope you know I expect you to treat her civilly, as you would any guest of ours. You're being so childish over this, I can hardly credit it. I was hurt too, but she is innocent. She was only three years old when it happened. She was told her mother died when she was a baby.'

'And naturally you believed her.'

'I always believe what I am told, unless I have good reason not to.'

'You have every reason not to. She's Louis Patrick's daughter. Brought up by him, influenced by him. Ask yourself, Laura, what can she be? Chris is wild but he wouldn't hurt a living thing, and do you know why? Because he was brought up to respect all living creatures. If our real mother had lived, I'd guarantee that Chris would be hunting whenever he could, thirsting after the fox's blood with the rest of them.'

'I fail to understand your reasoning, Damon.'

'Because you choose to.'

'Nevertheless, this is my home, too. Along with Chris and Robert, I am glad she's here.'

Rowan heard his fist thump down on some wooden surface. 'I fail to

113

understand how a woman of forty, married for fifteen years, can still be so naïve. Laura,' his voice softened considerably, 'your trustful nature is a wonderful thing despite it having irritated me at times before, but now you're just being stupid. Surely you don't believe that she came all the way here just to collect a few pieces of jewellery belonging to a mother she never knew. Louis Patrick must have bought her a king's ransom in jewellery over the years.'

'Why else would she come? Unless, of course, it was curiosity to see us, and even you, in this odd mood you're in, can't find fault with that. I was curious about her, too.'

'Perhaps you've forgotten that Louis Patrick owns a large slice of Allied Chemicals. They've been researching an anti-flu drug for years before we even started, and with bigger resources than we could ever hope for.'

'I don't see what that has to do with Rowan. We haven't even mentioned it to her.' Laura gave a little laugh. 'How could we? None of us are certain what it's about, anyway.'

'Laura,' he said in an exasperated voice that wasn't unkind, 'she'll know all about it already. Whatever precautions we take, rumours leak out and grow. Our rivals know what we are trying to do. What they don't know is the exact formula we're working on and how far we've gone with it. That letter was a heaven-sent opportunity for Patrick to try and find out through his daughter.'

'Now I *know* you're talking nonsense. She admitted that she hadn't told her father she was coming. He's away abroad at the moment and she had no way of contacting him before she came.'

'Well, she'd hardly admit that she had come with his blessing. I don't have to remind you what would happen if Louis Patrick discovered we're actually testing FU970 already. He tried to ruin us once and he's the sort of man who'd have a long memory, especially when the monetary advantage is so vast. If FU970 is successful it will mean a fortune to us, Laura. Enough in itself to tempt a man like Louis Patrick. And make no mistake, it could ruin us this time; the development of a drug like this one is a heavy commitment.'

'Oh, heavens,' Laura said tearfully, 'you make everything sound so sordid. I'm not convinced. Not at all, Damon. She'll have no opportunity to go anywhere near the factory. She's just seeing the district for a day or two . . .'

A noise behind her made Rowan swing round. 'Heard enough?' asked Chris in a hard, low voice from the stairs, and she knew he had heard at least part of the conversation.

She rushed over to him. She was near to tears herself. The conversation she had overheard had shocked her to the core of her being. 'Oh, Chris,' was all she could say for the moment.

He took her hands in his and the expression in his eyes softened. 'All right, Rowan, let's go in. He won't eat you.'

'But it's not true!'

'It doesn't matter if it is.'

She drew away. 'Don't you care?' she asked in amazement.

'I sold my shares. Foolish, wasn't it? Come along now, beard the tiger in his den.'

As Chris firmly took her arm and propelled her towards the door, Rowan had the oddest feeling that he was enjoying himself.

Laura started uneasily when they came in, but Rowan hardly noticed. She was shocked almost to the point of insensibility, but she wasn't too numb not to recognise the man who was standing in front of the empty fireplace. She had seen him twice before — once at The Duck and Gun and today in Kendal outside the dress shop.

'Where are your manners, Damon?' bantered Chris. 'Don't just stand there and stare, say hello to the lady.'

Rowan went straight over to Laura. She felt sick and was dismayed to find her legs were trembling, too. 'Laura, I heard something of what was said just now. I think it would be best if I left here immediately . . .'

Laura jumped to her feet. 'I won't hear of it, Rowan. My brother has had a shock in finding you here, that's all. He doesn't know what he's saying.'

'Just the same, I think . . .'

'I won't have you chased away like this,' Laura insisted, and Rowan was sorry to see that she was rapidly becoming upset.

'Damon sees industrial spies under every desk,' said Chris, grinning, 'just like the spinster sees a potential rapist under her bed.'

'We can do without flippant remarks from you,' his brother retorted, almost growling as he spoke.

Since Rowan had entered the room he had hardly taken his eyes from her face for a moment. He remained where he stood, his hands clasped behind his back and his face a mask of unrelieved severity.

'That's odd,' replied Chris easily, going to pour himself a drink, 'It's just what I thought you *did* need, before everyone starts getting really intense.'

'Laura,' Rowan burst out, unable to help herself, 'there is absolutely no truth in what your brother has suggested.' She cast a quick, withering look at the man in question. 'It's like something from the realms of cheap fiction.'

'It's a much more serious problem than that,' Damon answered in a surprisingly calm voice. 'A problem that is becoming increasingly difficult to solve. Taking precautions to defend our processes isn't just some idiosyncrasy of mine; it was decided upon by the whole board after several attempts to bribe our staff had been made. I traced one bribery attempt back to Allied Chemicals, although I couldn't prove it. There was even an attempted break-in.'

'Vandals,' Laura said quickly.

Damon shrugged in a way that was very much like Chris. Apart from that one characteristic they were quite unalike. Damon Halstead was much darker and of a heavier build than his brother. He was more like his sister, although where Laura's features were assembled in a way that was almost plain, the effect was quite a different one where Damon Halstead was concerned.

'Anyway,' Laura went on, her tone unusually firm, 'this is nothing to do with Rowan.'

'I didn't even know my father was connected with Allied Chemicals. He's never discussed business with me except in the most general way.' She turned, her anger mounting, to face Damon Halstead. 'I don't care what you think of my father. You have your reasons to dislike him which have nothing to do with your paltry discovery, but I can assure you he's too big a man to stoop so low as to do what you suggest, let alone send *me* to do the dirty work for him.'

His scornful and disbelieving grin heaped fuel on to her anger. 'Even to a 'big man' like Louis Patrick,' he said in a quiet voice, 'the prospect of having a commodity which might eventually be worth millions of pounds is no mean matter, to say nothing of the prestige involved.'

'I think you're letting your imagination run amok,' she retorted. 'This is what comes, Mr Halstead, of reading lurid fiction and watching too much television.'

To her satisfaction the grin disappeared and he looked at first surprised and then vexed. She knew very well that what she had suggested was the very last thing a man such as he would do.

Chris turned from the decanters, nursing his drink. 'You've got it wrong. It's Doctor Halstead. I can't tell you exactly what he's a doctor of because he has so many degrees I think that he's lost count himself, and if I did know I'm too ignorant to pronounce the words. Isn't that so, Damon?'

He looked hopefully at his brother, but Damon simply let out a gasp of exasperation, apparently at the light-hearted attitude his sister and his brother were adopting towards a matter he considered to be serious in the extreme.

Laura put her hand to her head. 'Oh, do stop this bickering, *please*. Thank goodness; here comes Robert.'

'Why on earth didn't *you* say something today?' Damon demanded the moment his brother-in-law came in.

'About what?' Robert asked in amazement.

'About Rowan being here,' Laura explained. 'He didn't know until this afternoon.'

Robert's face cleared. 'Oh, I thought you knew,' he said, smiling and obviously quite unaware of the tension in the room. He took the drink Chris had poured for him and sat down in a chair from which he could see everyone. Rowan could easily see why a placid fellow such as he should sometimes bring out the worst in Chris's sardonic sense of humour.

Robert sipped appreciatively at his drink and, realising that Damon was still waiting for an explanation, he said, 'We only exchanged a few words in the corridor, Damon. You said yourself that you were in a tearing hurry. There seemed no call to chat about something I thought you must already know.'

Chris winked at Rowan as she caught his eye and, seeing the gesture, Damon looked directly at her. 'All right, Miss Patrick, by all means stay here for as long as it suits you. If that is what the others want, so be it. I shall leave it to my brother to parade you around the area in royal style — I understand he's made a good start — but please don't expect me to act the hypocrite and welcome you here. The name of Patrick still leaves a bitter taste in my mouth.'

With that he marched out of the room. All the others stared after him. Robert was the first to speak. 'Good gracious,' he said, 'who'd have thought he would react like that.' He looked at his wife. 'I didn't know he still felt so badly about it, Laura.'

Laura flapped her hand impatiently. 'Oh, do be quiet, Robert. This is so unpleasant. If you can't say something constructive, keep quiet.'

It was, Rowan thought, one of the rare times that Laura Kingsley was out of patience.

'I think it might be best if I went,' she ventured.

Laura became alert. 'No, I'd never forgive myself if you left because of this. What an impression of us you must have.'

'No, really, you've all been marvellous. I understand, really I do.'

'You can't go because of Damon,' Chris told her. 'Surely he doesn't affect you to that extent.'

His choice of words, to Rowan's ears, was unfortunate. 'I think it might be best for you all,' she answered stiffly. 'I don't want to cause any unpleasantness in your family. It hardly matters to me when I leave, whether it's now or next week, but you all have to live together afterwards. That's *all* I meant.'

'I should think,' Robert put in mildly, 'that any unpleasantness you've caused has just been got over. There's nothing more to say on the matter.'

'Quite so,' Laura agreed. 'My brother has a fearful temper. When it's had time to cool a little he'll be more reasonable and see what a silly ass he's made of himself tonight.'

Rowan doubted it, but did not say so. She would give Laura the benefit of knowing her brother best. 'He's not a shallow person,' Laura went on, and Rowan noticed that almost involuntarily she looked to Chris. 'He feels things very deeply. Love or hate, it's intense.' She turned automatically towards the door. 'I wonder where he's gone.'

'I can hazard a guess,' her other brother answered as he poured himself another drink. 'He'll have gone to pour the whole sorry story into Carolyne's sympathetic ears, or, of course, he's rushed to double the guard on his bunsen burner. Come to think of it, he's probably done both.'

'Seriously, Rowan,' he went on, turning to her, 'he's far too well-mannered to put on another display like you've seen today. He'd have been good manners personified if you hadn't overheard what he was saying first. He'd have given you the freeze treatment, perhaps, but nothing more.'

'That's not the point . . . '

'Oh, come on, Rowan. He'll soon see he's wrong. Anyone who'd bolt like a frightened rabbit at a few harsh words could hardly be likened to Louis Patrick. Besides,' he added, downing his drink, 'you've promised to come with me to the dance on Friday.'

'Splendid!' Laura cried. 'Then there's no question of your leaving.'

Rowan felt trapped. She wheeled round on Chris. 'You must have known Damon would react like this when you asked me.'

Chris shrugged in a gesture that was characteristic of him.

'Oh, does it matter?' Laura asked quickly. 'I think we're all building this up out of all proportion to its importance. When we've eaten it won't seem half as bad. Do say you'll stay, Rowan. We all want it. Damon is hardly ever here. When he's not at the factory, he's at the Griffins'. You'll hardly see him. Oh dear, that isn't quite right. I'm so sorry.'

At the sight of Laura's distress Rowan's own irritation melted. She found she was comforting the older woman as if it were she who had been the recipient of Damon Halstead's wrath.

'Don't be upset about it, Laura; of course I'm staying. I came here with the best of intentions and couldn't have had a nicer reception. I've bought a new dress today,' she added with feminine logic, 'and I'm not being done out of wearing it.'

5

Rowan was awake early the next morning. She had spent a restless night. Sleep had been elusive and when it did come it had been interrupted by vivid dreams of a man who looked at her alternately with admiration and hatred.

From where she lay in the bed the chiffon evening dress was constantly before her eyes, mocking her in its elegance. She knew she would gain precious little joy from wearing it now. Had it not been for Laura's very real distress Rowan would have packed her suitcase and left first thing this morning. But for Laura's sake she could not go, and Rowan had the oddest feeling that she would come to regret her decision.

In direct contrast to the previous morning, today Rowan was hesitant to go down to breakfast, fearful of bumping into the man who had haunted her dreams. When at last the knock came at her door she was dressed and ready to go down, glad of Chris's company.

'It's a lovely morning,' he announced. 'Someone up above must be smiling on this visit of yours, Rowan. We can have a leisurely day seeing the sights.'

'I had hoped to make a start on the painting, Chris.'

'Later. You can't escape me so easily. I have a better idea — compromise. There seems no point in my having a half-share in a riding school if one doesn't take advantage of the facilities. Skelvingsdale is as pretty as any village in the Lake District. We can spend the morning jogging round. Does that appeal to you?'

Immediately the prospect cheered her. 'It certainly does! I haven't been on a horse since I was at school, though,' she warned him.

'You'll soon get into your stride again. Don't worry, we'll get you a placid mount. They're used to absolute beginners.'

As they approached the premises of the school Rowan was again apprehensive. She felt a sudden reluctance to meet Carolyne Griffin. The girl was unavoidably coupled in her mind with Damon Halstead. But she need not have worried; Carolyne had not yet arrived. The stable girl in charge brought out their mounts and in a very short time Rowan was once more at ease in the saddle.

The rest of the morning passed pleasantly. After returning to Skelvingsdale Hall for lunch, Rowan unpacked her equipment and Chris helped her to carry it down the hill.

It was not entirely to her satisfaction that he settled back to stay with her. She would have preferred to be alone for a while. However much he was out of the house, she was very much aware of the necessity of facing Damon Halstead again, and she badly needed time to arm herself for that eventuality.

However, when Chris began to realise that it was not just a matter of a few quick strokes, but something which required painstaking care, he grew restless and to Rowan's relief decided to take Hamish the long way home by way of the village.

He left her alone with her thoughts; thoughts of a man who loved and hated intensely. Rowan didn't doubt it. She wondered if he loved Carolyne Griffin intensely. If he did, she asked herself, would he be content to let their lives drift in this way?

The sun had moved — or, rather, the earth's position in relation to it had — and the light was no longer good. However, she reckoned she had done a good day's work and the results were satisfactory. She packed up her equipment and returned to the house.

★ ★ ★

It came as something of a shock when she walked into the sitting room a little later to find Damon Halstead the only other occupant.

He was sitting in a chair with a drink in his hand, facing the door, so that there was no chance of her making a discreet withdrawal before she was noticed.

She experienced yet another surprise when he smiled and said mildly, 'Come along in, Rowan. There's nothing to be frightened of — really. I gave up eating young women when they started to give me indigestion.'

Sheepishly she smiled when she realised what a foolish sight she must have presented, ready to bolt like the frightened rabbit Chris had likened her to.

Hamish was lying by the side of Damon's chair, whose free hand was caressing the animal's ear. As she came in Damon got to his feet and Hamish looked at her resentfully.

'May I pour you a drink?'

Feeling that keeping her wits firmly about her was more necessary than courage a drink may give her, Rowan refused. He subsided into the chair again. He was at ease. His anger and resentment were no longer evident, but she didn't doubt that it was still there. She had armed herself against his further anger, so this mildness towards her only served to disconcert her further.

She walked across the room to the window where she could look out at the peaceful view and not at him.

'It looks very much as if you've decided to stay,' he said a few moments later.

The chink of ice against the glass as he poured himself another drink grated. 'Yes, I have. I can see no good reason why I shouldn't. My conscience is clear.' He looked at her steadily and her confidence wavered. 'I'd promised Laura . . . '

'Even though you might ultimately do her harm?'

She turned round then. Even Hamish was aware of the sudden tension in the air. His head came up, his ears alert.

'So you persist in believing I have some ulterior motive in coming here?'

Instead of returning to his chair he came across to stand by her side. 'Wonderful view, isn't it? I sometimes have this frightening dream; that one day, when we're all dead and gone, Skelvingsdale Hall will be an hotel filled with gaping tourists.'

She knew he was joking, and that it was probably aimed at her, which annoyed her further. She glared at him. He studied her carefully for a moment or two and then he said, 'I mean gossip, Rowan. You know what that is, of course, but you don't know what it can be like in a small community like ours. My sister lives for the community. She is respected and she has earned that respect. There are many people living around here who still remember that old scandal, and before you remind me, I know it was Laura who asked you here, but my sister is an extremely generous woman. She is also a woman who does what she believes is right even though it may not be in her own best interests.

'Now that you've turned up, and after it's taken twenty years of living down that scandal, it's all going to start up again.'

'It certainly will if you are a typical resident of this village,' she retorted. 'It's a great pity you all have nothing more important to concern you.'

She turned away from him quite deliberately and he went across to the table, absently rearranging the glasses standing on it. 'I can remember the taunts we got then.' He glanced across at her. 'And I can remember Laura's tears. She's not a child any more, but she can be hurt just as easily as she was then.'

Rowan bit her lip. She turned round and gripped the back of one of the chairs tightly. 'If there is any gossip, it will be critical of *me*, no one else. I didn't turn up for the first time until weeks after her funeral, and then only for what she left me. What will the gossips make of that?'

The door opened again to admit Laura and Robert. Laura stared anxiously at them both, and when Damon smiled and went to her, her face relaxed.

Although Rowan had enjoyed her previous meals at Skelvingsdale Hall, tonight she picked at the trout which had been caught locally.

'I shall have to go fishing again,' Chris commented as it was served. 'It's years since I brought home a catch for our supper.' He looked at Rowan. 'I used to enjoy a day of relaxation by a lake or a river. We used to go regularly; do you remember, Damon?'

'I wish I had the time.'

'You had the time then. I remember when you once kept one fish back for yourself. You wanted to cut it up to find out how it worked. Do you still do that? I often wonder.'

Rowan felt uncomfortable. Damon was an easygoing butt for Chris's humour, as were Laura and Robert, but it seemed that Damon's anger was tightly under control this evening, and it would take very little goading for it to be released and this uneasy truce to end.

But he simply looked across at his brother and said mildly, 'I've grown up since then, Chris. It's only a pity you haven't.'

All the meat and dairy foods that came to the house were from local farms, and Mrs Jennings, although she possessed a prosaic appearance, was a very good cook. Tonight, though, to Rowan, it all tasted like ashes.

Chris and Laura kept up an almost non-stop conversation between them while Damon seemed quite at ease, happy to listen to them and contribute a comment where required. Robert was content to concentrate on his food and as usual spoke infrequently.

Laura was more talkative than ever, which Rowan attributed to her having her elder brother home and because there had been an apparent end to the unpleasantness. If she sensed constraint in the atmosphere she certainly did not indicate it by word or gesture. Rowan, now that she was coming to know the woman better, could easily credit the agonies she must have suffered at that sensitive age when the full publicity of scandal had fallen upon them.

'Did you find your way back without any difficulty this afternoon, Rowan?' Laura asked as Rowan bravely attempted to tackle Mrs Jennings's sweet concoction of strawberries, mousse and cream. 'I was quite worried when I saw Chris return without you, and he just wouldn't say where you'd gone.'

Chris and Rowan exchanged glances and she said to him in a soft voice, 'There's no secret, Chris. Laura is going to see me carrying a wopping canvas around, so, unfortunately, it can't be kept as a surprise.'

'What are you two whispering about?' Laura asked.

Damon was looking at them both

with interest, and Rowan wondered if he suspected her of donning a mask and gloves and creeping around the countryside, seeking opportunities of stealing his formula, aided and abetted by Chris. At the thought of it she smiled to herself and as she looked up she caught his eye and immediately felt foolish. Since yesterday she had come to a reluctant conclusion that Damon Halstead was not given to hysterical or angry outbursts without good reason, and the fact that he must be truly anxious about her presence worried her more than she was willing to admit to herself.

'Rowan is doing a picture for you,' Chris explained when, for no reason she could name, her own voice failed to function.

Laura's eyes opened wide, first in surprise and then pleasure. 'A picture for me?'

Robert laughed. 'That's unexpected, Laura,' he murmured. 'How very nice,' and then he returned to his sweet.

'What kind of a picture?' she asked, still surprised.

Rowan was aware that Damon's eyes were on her. It was amazing that just by his presence he would make her every word and action seem to have a guilty connotation.

Determined not to let him fluster her further, she turned to look at Laura. 'The view from the bottom of the hill, of this house, is so good that I decided to have a shot at painting it — providing the weather keeps fine. I should manage it before I leave. Two or three sessions from the bottom of the hill should be enough, and if necessary I can finish it indoors. I know the effect I'm trying to achieve. The house is very much like a giant bird in its eyrie. That's what I shall try to convey on to canvas.'

'How clever!' Laura beamed. 'And you really want to give it to *me*, Rowan?'

'Of course. It's little enough for the hospitality you've given *me*.' She deliberately kept her eyes averted from Damon.

'But, my dear,' Laura protested, 'you've not come here to spend all your time doing something for me. I want you to go out and enjoy yourself.'

'I'm painting it for my own pleasure. I've always wanted to do that, and seeing that view gives me all the incentive I need. Being out there in the valley, I shall get lots of fresh air and the climb up and down the path will provide me with much-needed exercise. I don't get nearly enough when I'm at home. It's so much easier to slip into the car.'

'May I see how far you've got with it?' Laura asked like a child anxious for a promised treat.

'I'd rather you wait until it's finished, Laura.'

'Perhaps that would be best,' the woman admitted, but her disappointment was evident.

'From what I've seen of it,' Chris told his sister, 'it's jolly good.'

Rowan smiled her appreciation at his flattery, which was obviously sincere, and Laura looked in earnest at her elder brother. 'It's quite remarkable, this, Damon; Delia once said that she would have liked to have been an artist if she'd had the chance.'

Damon gave Rowan a scathing glance. 'She always had far too much to do to indulge her own fancies.'

Rowan's fury seethed away inside her. He was peeling and quartering a peach with clinical precision. Laura laughed, a little uncomfortably, and said, 'Is that for me, dear?' He handed it over to her on the plate, and she said to Rowan, 'I always make a mess over everything if I do it myself.'

'As a matter of fact,' Rowan said, addressing herself to Damon who was peeling another peach and appeared not to be listening, 'I haven't had the time to indulge my fancy and paint for my own pleasure since I was at school.'

When Damon looked up he was

surprised. 'Why ever not? Don't you sit around all day daubing canvasses for Daddy's serfs to come and admire?'

So Damon had that irritating cynical streak in him too, Rowan thought. Her eyes narrowed with the glint of battle. She had tried to show herself in a good light; she was tired of being mild and apologetic in his company. 'No, I certainly do not. I don't have to work, I admit. My father didn't want me to and we had several arguments on the subject.' Realising that she was being rude in addressing Damon solely, and not being able to hold his gaze any longer, she turned to include the others. 'I spent a year in a French finishing school to keep him happy, and after that I had my way and went to art school.'

'Not on a grant,' Chris interrupted, and when he grinned she couldn't be angry with him.

She didn't pause to wonder why Chris's sarcasm should make her smile whilst Damon's only angered her.

'Not on a grant,' she answered with a smile.

'What kind of work do you do?' It was Laura who spoke. 'I never imagined you would do anything. One always reads of these young women who ski and sail and go to balls because they need do nothing else.'

'I do all that too,' she admitted. 'I work for myself the rest of the time — free-lance.' She shot a glance at Damon. 'And I've managed to support myself very well since I left college.'

'Don't you live with your father any more?' Robert asked, having finished his meal.

'No.' She looked down at the plate in front of her. 'He leads a very active social life. He never let me hinder him in it, but, all the same, he's freer now I've gone. I still come and go as I please. Most of my belongings are still at his flat, but I love my little studio. I'm Rowan Patrick there, not Louis Patrick's daughter. There's a difference, as you can imagine.' She looked up

144

again, feeling slightly embarrassed. 'We meet regularly when he's in Town. I think we have an even better relationship now.'

'We always imagined you differently — quite different,' Laura said thoughtfully, and Rowan flushed slightly.

Damon sat forward, his hands clasped in front of him on the table. 'Delia always said, and it was the only thing that worried her, that your father would mould you to his ways.'

'I'm sure that's true,' she answered. 'We are all moulded by our parents. In my case it must be my father, although I spent most of my childhood away from him at school, so, following that idea, it's possible I'm also like my art mistress who was, now I come to think of her, a quietly repressed spinster of about forty-five. She saw nothing of the outside world except for the long summer holiday when she visited her married sister and spent the entire six weeks teaching her three nieces to draw.'

A laugh rippled round the room and to Rowan's relief the atmosphere, which had threatened to turn stormy, lightened.

'Well, you've certainly inherited his spirit,' said Laura, and then disparagingly, 'If it can be called that in his case.'

Rowan looked directly at Damon. He was frowning. Perhaps it was, she thought, because he had failed to disconcert her. 'And do you think I've inherited all his other qualities?' she challenged.

He allowed himself a small smile. 'I should think you, too, can have anything you set your mind on,' he answered.

She looked away quickly. I wonder, she thought; I really wonder.

'What sort of things do you do?' Laura asked quickly. 'You didn't tell us.'

Rowan felt suddenly dispirited. 'Anything. Anything I'm asked. Last year, for instance, I was asked to design carpets and curtains for a house that was being built. The owner wanted his initials included in the pattern, yet he didn't want the same pattern all over the house.'

She was discovering that while she was speaking of a matter with which she was totally familiar she wasn't so aware of Damon's disconcerting presence, and she prattled on.

'It was the hardest job I've ever undertaken; I had to work in conjunction with the architect and the interior decorator. It was hard, but fun, and the customer was satisfied. In fact, I had a write-up in *Modern Interiors*. After that I was never short of work, but I only accept commissions that I want to do, and then I give friends priority.'

'Which means you will never be out of work,' Damon remarked, 'because I'm sure your father's contacts will make sure you're kept going.'

She looked at him again. 'I've done a great deal of work for my father's friends, but they are invariably people who can afford the best and they certainly expect value for money. I have the satisfaction of knowing I earn my money. If you are ever in London I'd be glad to show you some examples of my work.'

'Wait till you see her masterpiece, Damon,' Chris told him. 'It's good, and coming from someone who wouldn't know a Rembrandt from a piece of kitchen wallpaper, that's praise.'

Damon didn't appear particularly anxious to see the painting, and it gave Rowan a perverse pleasure to know that Laura would almost certainly display it prominently once it was finished. Damon would be forced to look at it whenever he came into the house.

Chris glanced at her and there was mischief in his manner. 'When you marry this architect fellow of yours you'll be able to go into some kind of partnership.'

'Getting married!' exclaimed Laura. 'How marvellous. When will it be?'

Rowan was angry. She wished Chris

hadn't mentioned her coming engagement. She didn't know why she wanted no mention made of it, only that it was so.

'I don't know,' she murmured, her eyes downcast. 'Nothing is definite yet.'

Damon pushed back his chair in an abrupt gesture. 'You'll have to excuse me; I have to go out.'

Rowan watched him go — to Carolyne? she wondered. A man who was so implacable in his hatred could also be ardent in love.

The dining room door slammed rather loudly. Laura began to get up. Rowan guessed that she was now slightly more relaxed. She looked round at them all and smiled broadly. 'Well, I suppose we'd better go and have our coffee in the sitting room . . . '

6

Chris left for Manchester the next morning, where there were several cars he wanted to see. He invited Rowan to accompany him, but she refused and handed him the keys of her own car for his use, which seemed to satisfy him.

The day dawned sunny and she could not be sorry Chris was going to be away. She found him good company, but constantly that company tended to become cloying. His intentions towards her were not serious, of this she was convinced, yet he wanted her to spend almost every waking hour with him, and this she was reluctant to do. Even the previous evening, after Damon had gone so abruptly, when she should have been able to relax, she had felt oddly dispirited instead.

Today, with both brothers out of the way and the sun shining in the cloudless sky, she was determined to press on with the painting. She set up her equipment and tried to concentrate on the canvas, but she could not stop herself from thinking.

Her decision to stay was not because of her promise to Chris, for Laura's sake, or even in spite of Damon. She realised now that it was for none of these reasons.

She liked Laura, certainly; she liked her very much indeed, but the woman would have understood her desire to leave Skelvingsdale after that first distressing confrontation with Damon. In fact, it would have been the only sensible thing to do. And she certainly couldn't be held to her promise to Chris, for he had known, or at least suspected, what Damon's reaction to her coming would be.

There was something more than the reasons she had given herself drawing her to this place, and that something was an elusive factor.

The morning passed quickly and

Rowan was satisfied with her progress. She returned to the house at lunchtime and, despite Laura's lighthearted pleas, returned the canvas unseen to her room.

Only Laura and Rowan were present for lunch, which, as the main meal of the day was in the evening, only consisted of cold meat and salad, followed by fresh fruit and cream. They took coffee outside on the terrace.

'It's very fortunate you came when the weather shows the countryside to its best advantage,' Laura said.

'I should think it's beautiful in all seasons. The snow must look lovely on the fells.'

Laura laughed. 'It *looks* lovely, but it can be a darned nuisance!' She poured second cups of coffee. 'I don't like to ask because I so enjoy having you here, but when do you intend to go home?'

'After the dance.'

'You'd better leave it until Sunday. You'll be in no fit state to drive all that way on Saturday. We all relax on the day after. Breakfast is usually served around lunchtime.'

'Then Sunday it is.'

Laura looked at her again as she stirred her coffee thoughtfully. 'Will you come again, Rowan?'

For a moment she didn't answer. She didn't know how. She was going home to Tony and she knew he wouldn't sanction a visit, be it with or without him. And then there was Daddy. Rowan felt cold at the thought of facing him with her knowledge. She could hardly envisage visiting Skelvingsdale again in the wake of their disapproval. And then, of course, Damon wouldn't want her.

'It might be difficult,' she said at last, 'if I'm to be married . . . '

'If.' What a silly thing to have said. 'When' was what she should have said.

Laura leaned over and patted her hand. 'I understand, but if you and your husband-to-be ever want to come, you're welcome.'

Rowan smiled her thanks. She knew she never would. 'I had a daughter,'

Laura said a moment later. Rowan looked at her with interest, and Laura smiled sadly. 'She was born eight weeks prematurely and died two days later. After that there were no more; I don't know why. She would have just been coming into her teens now. It seems fantastic, when I think of it now, that I might have been the mother of a teenage daughter. I think sometimes your mother felt like that when she thought of you.'

'Oh, I *am* sorry, Laura.'

The woman got to her feet quickly and smiled. 'I don't think about it very often now. I don't think she did, either.'

'I must hurry along, Rowan. There's a meeting of an institute I belong to at Harvington. I always attend. Will you be all right on your own? You can come along if you wish, only you'd be bored silly.'

Rowan laughed. 'You run along, Laura. I intended to go down to the village and beg a horse from the stables.'

The thought had, in fact, only just popped into her head, but it seemed a good idea. 'After all these years I've rediscovered a liking for riding.'

Rowan, however, found herself walking slowly towards the village. Yesterday only the stable girl was there; today Carolyne Griffin herself might be present, and Rowan was strangely nervous of meeting her.

The courtyard was deserted when she went through the archway and round the back of The Duck and Gun where the horses were stabled. In one of the stalls a horse whinneyed. Rowan walked hesitantly, almost on tip-toe. And then, realising she was being silly, she slipped her hands into the pockets of her jeans and shouted, 'Hello, there. Is anyone about?'

A moment later Carolyne Griffin appeared. She came out of one of the stalls, hurrying at first, and then she checked abruptly when she saw Rowan. She stared at her and Rowan said, rather daunted by Carolyne's unsmiling appearance, 'Good afternoon. I'm Rowan Patrick. Chris Halstead . . . '

'I know who you are,' the girl answered. 'What is it you want?'

Rowan struggled to retain her smiling composure. 'I'd like to hire one of your mounts. Chris said I may any time I wish. We came yesterday — I don't know whether the girl told you. I had Domino as my mount.'

'Domino is out. They're all out this morning.'

It was obvious that Damon had very successfully passed on his prejudice to his girlfriend. The girl's appearance couldn't have been more unfriendly. For a moment Rowan was inclined to retire gracefully, and then her old fighting spirit came to the fore. Chris Halstead owned half of the business, and Carolyne had no right to turn away custom whatever were her private feelings.

'Then perhaps I could have another mount.'

The girl's eyes narrowed slightly.

'Domino is usually used for beginners. Are you a beginner?'

Rowan was glad to be able to say, 'No,' adding, 'But I'm out of practice. I haven't ridden for some years.'

Carolyne hesitated a moment. 'All right, then. I'll saddle my own mare. She should suit you.'

'If you're sure . . . ' Rowan began.

The girl had turned away already, but she shot over her shoulder, smiling for the first time, 'Why not? You are a friend of Chris's, after all, and for your cheek in coming you deserve something.'

Rowan gasped. 'Just one minute!' she demanded, and the girl checked. 'I won't bother today, thank you.'

Carolyne turned round. She was still smiling, but there was no warmth in her manner. 'No doubt you're just aching to rush off to tell Chris that I've been difficult. Well, Miss Rowan Patrick, I'm not giving you a chance to make mischief for me. I'll saddle Daisy. I presume you *did* come to ride?'

Without giving Rowan a chance to reply, she went back into the stall. Not that Rowan could have spoken at that moment; she was quite speechless, although she derived some grim satisfaction from the realisation that Carolyne and Damon were well suited. They were both bad-mannered, ill-tempered and totally intolerant, but it shocked her, too, to realise that she actually expected to dislike Carolyne Griffin.

To Rowan's relief it was the stable girl who led out the chestnut mare a few minutes later. The animal was bigger than the one she had ridden the previous day, and one that was obviously from a good stud, and Rowan looked at her a little apprehensively. The girl handed over the bridle and Rowan ran her hand along the mare's flank, speaking to her softly as she did so. Daisy responded by giving a rapturous snicker in Rowan's ear.

'She likes you,' said the stable girl. 'She don't take to everyone, bein' as she's Miss Griffin's 'orse. You should see them together. They ride like one, they do. There ain't any of the trials that Miss Griffin 'asn't won at some time or other.'

'She must be a very fine horse-woman,' Rowan murmured.

She had put off the moment when she must mount, feeling, somehow, that she might fall flat on her face in front of Carolyne Griffin, but she could postpone it no longer. After checking the girths carefully, she thrust her foot into the stirrup and swung into the saddle.

Patting the mare gently, she sat back in the saddle. She already felt at home. The mare was obviously well-trained and mild-natured.

'You haven't got a hard hat,' Carolyne pointed out from where she stood watching, by the stable door.

'Do I need one?'

'It's always best, but, as you say, you're not a beginner,' she answered, and went back into the stall.

Rowan urged Daisy forward. She had

no idea where she was going to go on Daisy; the urge to ride had suddenly dissolved in the face of Carolyne Griffin's unpleasantness, but she supposed she had no choice but to take Daisy out now.

The horse had taken her only a few yards down the main street, past The Duck and Gun, when she began to buck slightly. With a fast-beating heart, Rowan tried to steady her, but the more she patted and crooned to the mare the more she bucked. Suddenly, as a car came round the corner, Daisy reared into the air and Rowan, in retrospect, didn't really know how she managed to keep her seat.

The car drew up, its brakes squealing so loudly it was almost deafening. She clung desperately to the animal's neck as a familiar voice, in an unfamiliar tone, murmured soothing sounds into her ear. After a few moments — the longest Rowan could ever recall — the animal, mercifully, quietened down and Rowan opened her eyes. She slid to the ground and was steadied by a strong hand.

'Are you all right?'

She looked at Damon at last, took a deep breath and nodded. 'Is your car all right?'

'Oh, hang the car! What do you think you're about bringing Daisy on to the road?'

'Why shouldn't I?' she asked him in surprise. 'Where else should I go?'

'Daisy shouldn't be ridden along the road. She was involved in a motor accident some weeks ago — a drunken driver careered through the village — and now she reacts violently whenever she sees or hears a car. Didn't the girl tell you? Wait until . . . '

'Miss Griffin saddled her for me.'

His hand remained tightly clasped around her arm as he led both Rowan and Daisy back towards the stables. Vaguely, Rowan was aware that curious faces had appeared at several doors to the cottages across the road, and those who had been in The Duck and Gun had come out to see what all the noise was about.

Carolyne's face was a picture of dismay when she saw them come into the courtyard.

'What has happened?' she asked.

'My car frightened her and she tried to throw Rowan.'

Carolyne rushed up to her horse and pressed her face against Daisy's head. 'Oh, poor Daisy,' she said. 'What a dreadful thing to happen.'

'Poor Daisy!' Damon cried, and Rowan realised his temper was very near to breaking. 'Don't you realise that a serious accident almost happened just now? It's lucky my car has good brakes or we'd both be on our way to 'General' and heaven knows what might have happened to Daisy this time. She was lucky to escape without a scratch last time. This horse must have a charmed life.

'What I fail to understand is why you didn't warn Rowan not to take Daisy out on to the road. As a stranger, she would hardly go any other way.'

Carolyne's eyes opened ingenuously. She handed the horse's bridle to the stable girl, who led her away, and then stood with her hands tucked into the top of her jodhpurs. 'I did tell her. Of course I did. I would be dangerously negligent if I didn't.'

'You did not!' Rowan retorted, at last shocked out of the stupor into which the near-accident had put her.

'I most certainly did. You're so arrogant and sure of yourself you just didn't listen to me.' She turned to Damon. 'She's just making excuses. Darling, is it likely I'd jeopardise my animal?'

Damon looked from one to the other. 'No,' he answered at last, 'I don't suppose you would.' He took Rowan's arm again. 'Well, it's done, and thank goodness no one has come to any harm. There's no point in having an enquiry now. Come along, Rowan, I'll take you back home.' He gave her a critical glance. 'In future you should try and listen to what you are told. On this occasion it was in your own interest.'

She tried to pull away from him, unsuccessfully. 'It isn't true, Damon,' she said in anguish, using his name for the first time. 'She didn't tell me.'

'You probably didn't hear,' he answered with surprising gentleness. 'You're in no state to remember just now.'

'Is it so impossible for you to believe *me*?'

'I don't disbelieve you. You simply did not hear. It can easily happen.'

Rowan no longer cared. What did it matter if she had been told or not? She allowed him to draw her away from Carolyne, but not before she had seen the malicious gleam in the girl's eye. That in itself settled any query she might have had.

As they went across the courtyard Carolyne darted after them. 'Damon, will I see you tonight?'

'I don't know,' he answered without looking at her. 'Don't rely on it.'

Carolyne's face flushed slightly and her expression was fierce, but her voice was soft as she said, 'It doesn't matter if it's late, Damon. Come when you can. I'll be waiting for you.'

Rowan hardly knew what was happening to her as she was gently put into the car. The last few minutes had passed in something of a fog.

'I'm putting you to a great deal of trouble,' she heard herself saying.

'Don't bother yourself about that. Try to relax while I get you home.' She was aware that he was frowning. 'Rowan, are you sure you're not hurt?'

'No, I'm all right,' she answered, unaware that her voice was nowhere near steady. 'Thanks to you. If you hadn't been so prompt in stopping and steadying Daisy I might easily have been hurt; so might you.'

He started up the engine and backed the car into the yard of The Duck and Gun. 'Let's not think of what might have happened.'

But she couldn't help but think of it.

She might so easily have been thrown from the horse, perhaps under the wheels of Damon's car. Carolyne must have known that at least one car was sure to come along and that it was certain to panic Daisy. Carolyne had known that the horse was almost sure to throw her mount and she had deliberately refrained from warning Rowan to keep away from the road.

Rowan laid her head back on the seat. The leather was cool; just what she needed. She wasn't thinking very clearly but enough to realise that Carolyne had deliberately tried to engineer an accident. She had suggested Daisy, almost insisted upon her riding the mare, but if there had been an accident to Rowan, Carolyne could not have been held responsible in any way, yet Rowan's injuries would have been just as serious.

The knowledge made her start to tremble. She was hardly aware of reaching the house and being helped out of the car. In the hall Hamish came bounding up to them hopefully. Involuntarily, Rowan flinched away from him and, taking his collar, Damon shut the dog out of the sitting room.

'A good strong brandy is what you need, my girl,' he said briskly, going across to the table where the drinks were set out, and she wondered why he was being so nice to her.

She sank down on to one of the sofas. 'I hate brandy,' she murmured. 'I'd far rather have a double scotch just now.'

One dark eyebrow rose slightly before he set out two glasses. 'I think I shall join you.' He stood over her while she drank it, the glass clasped tightly in her hands. Although she felt dazed, she was not too badly shocked not to be conscious of him.

'Another?' he asked when she had finished.

She shook her head. It was beginning to clear. 'That is quite enough, thank you. I feel much better now.'

He studied her carefully for a

moment or two. 'Yes, you look it. When you came in, your face was the same shade of green as the curtains. I always did think they were rather a sickly shade. Shock should never be treated lightly.'

She laughed although she still felt slightly shaky. 'If it hadn't been for you I might still be wandering around the village in a daze.'

He sat down next to her and involuntarily she moved further away, yet he gave no sign that he had noticed her action. 'What a fearful thought,' he said, finishing off his drink. 'Still, it would have given those overworked tongues in the village something new to talk about.'

He stared ahead as if he were deep in thought, and she took the opportunity to study his face carefully. 'You shouldn't be in research, you know. You'd make a very good M.D. I didn't know I was suffering from shock.'

He looked amused. 'Of course you didn't, but I could see it. There's nothing very clever about it.'

'No, but you've a good bedside manner when you're so inclined.'

'You don't know me very well, obviously. I couldn't possibly be happy treating adolescents for acne and their mothers for backache.'

'There's more to it than that.'

'More tedium. I couldn't bear it. I think I'd probably treat most of the patients by booting them out of the surgery. No, I'm very happy doing what I do, even though some of the locals believe I'm developing germ bombs, and Chris would have you believe I'm some *enfant terrible*.' He smiled slightly to himself. 'Contrary to anything he might have told you, I don't pay the local undertaker to snatch bodies for my vile experiments.'

Rowan laughed. 'Has he really said that? He hasn't gone so far as to say that to me, but it does sound like one of his remarks. He's quite incorrigible, but I like him for it.'

The way he was looking at her was

disconcerting; everything he did served to discompose her. 'I should say, knowing Chris better than most, that he likes you, too.'

She was still holding her empty glass tightly in her hand. She rubbed her thumb absently along the pattern cut into its rim. 'Damon, do you really believe I have an ulterior motive in coming here?'

He slid his arm along the back of the sofa. 'I can't think of a likelier one. Think of it from my point of view. I don't think you're desperate for the jewellery, you don't appear to be overly sentimental — and curious? Yes, I suppose you were curious to see us, to see where your mother was living all those years. That's natural enough.' He frowned at the carpet. 'So is this little errand on your father's behalf? I'd do the same if I were in your position, Rowan.'

He looked at her. 'Did you have a good look at the factory when you passed? Yes, of course you did.' She

170

looked down at her empty glass again and she knew he was smiling. 'You'll have seen the tractors clearing the land. When you tell your father about it he'll know we're making room for an extension to the factory and draw his own conclusion as to the reason. You'll have something to report when you go home, Rowan, but it won't really be what is needed, will it? I don't mind you seeing what we're doing to the factory; I'm very proud of the advances we've made since I joined the firm.'

'How can you be sure your rivals aren't even more advanced in producing this kind of drug?'

If she had hoped to ruffle his maddening calm she was disappointed. 'The same way they get their information. Actually, I find it all quite amusing. They have such big resources, but then, of course, it's all so impersonal, too. The research staff in all probability never see their board of directors, so it all takes that much longer.'

'While, here, you are one of the directors.'

'It helps. It definitely helps.' He looked at her. 'There can't be a home in the land that doesn't contain several examples of Allied Chemicals. Every synthetic fibre — even the sweater you're wearing — is pioneered and produced by them; almost everything manufactured has some component made by them, yet the thought of some small concern like ours finally producing a drug that's effective against all types of flu viruses evokes all their power to beat us to it. But they won't, you know. They most certainly won't.'

'I can understand your anxiety, and theirs. It's a matter of pounds, shillings and pence, or I should say pounds and pence. Big companies are like monsters with an ever-ready appetite for money and power.' He looked at her and she couldn't read his expression. 'Personally,' she said more boldly, 'I would rather spend a few days in bed when I get flu.'

'But, then, you are able to — in comfort. And no doubt take a Continental holiday to disperse the ill-effects. Make no mistake about it,' he added more seriously, 'once there is a successful anti-flu drug on the market we're only steps away from curing the common cold, and scientists have been chasing that particular rainbow for an awful long time.'

'You're remarkably calm about my being here.'

'There's no reason why I shouldn't be. You've learned little that they didn't already know, and I'm going to make sure you won't learn anything more. It's not my habit to make scenes, Rowan. I was caught off-balance the other night. It's been a hard struggle keeping FU970 a secret for so long. So, as you can imagine, it came as quite a shock to find you here in my own home.'

'Yes, I can imagine that,' she said quietly. 'Well, I won't be here to trouble you for much longer.'

He kept on looking at her steadily.

'You don't trouble me.'

A car was approaching the house. Rowan heard it stop and the door slam. All the time she held his gaze, puzzled as to what she could see there in his eyes.

The door to the sitting room opened abruptly. Laura beamed at the sight of them both, sitting in apparent harmony together. 'What on earth are you doing here, Damon? And Rowan,' she said before he had a chance to answer, 'I thought you were going riding this afternoon.'

Damon got to his feet, replacing his empty glass on the table as he did so. He smiled at his sister, gave her a quick kiss on the cheek and said, 'Rowan will explain. She's very good at it.'

7

As the week drew to a close the weather remained fine and Rowan was determined to finish the painting before she left for London, for it was turning out far better than she had dared to hope. Chris, at last, accepted that she was not willing to chase around the county with him and consoled himself by using her car in the search for a new one of his own.

One afternoon Rowan agreed to accompany Laura to the church to see the family plot, although she was not altogether keen to go.

'I come every week to put fresh flowers on it,' Laura explained, 'not just for Delia, but for them all. There's quite a few generations of Halsteads here. My mother's here, too, of course, and my father.'

The plot was well-kept, and as Laura

placed the flowers on it Rowan was uncomfortable. She had come only to please Laura and it was as if she were committing an act of sacrilege in doing so. Being here meant nothing to her. She still thought of her mother as having died twenty years ago, and as far as Rowan was concerned, she had.

Afterwards Laura pointed out a few of her ancestors. 'That's my great-aunt Myra. It's said that she died of unrequited love, but as she was seventy-eight when she went I doubt if that's really true. That's William Halstead, and I'm told that he was quite a character, too — rather eccentric. He had an obsession, I'm told, that everyone he met was out to steal his money. His will gave his heirs detailed instructions how to safeguard the family cash!'

'Rather like Damon,' Rowan murmured drily, 'only he thinks everyone is out to steal his formula.'

Laura laughed a little uncomfortably. 'There are quite a few people who would like the chance. And talking of chance,' she went on quickly, obviously anxious to change the subject, 'I must go and have a few words with Mrs Alexander while I'm here — she's the vicar's wife. It won't take me more than a few minutes.'

'I'll wait here for you.'

'Are you sure?' Laura frowned. 'I'm certain Mrs Alexander would be delighted to see you.'

'No, I'd really prefer to stay out here alone for a while.'

Laura gave her a smile of understanding. 'All right, I'll be back soon.'

She hurried off down the path. She had misunderstood Rowan's reasons, but it didn't matter.

Rowan began to walk slowly up and down. It was a small churchyard and very picturesque — the type tourists came to see all summer. She occupied herself by reading the inscriptions on the headstones. Suddenly a voice, saying, 'Hello, there,' made her gasp.

She whirled round. Damon was on

the path outside. His height dwarfed the wall on which he was leaning so negligently.

'Do you make a habit of haunting graveyards?' she asked coldly.

'Only when my fellow ghosts are so interesting.'

She turned away again. Her composure was always uncertain when he was around, never more so than now. He insulted her and despised her, yet there was a quality about him that undeniably attracted her, too. Perhaps it was because, although she had met men equally as arrogant and dynamic as he, there was never one who resisted her charms quite so well.

'How did you know I was here?' she asked as casually as she could.

'I didn't,' he admitted, 'but I saw Laura's car outside. Although,' he added, 'when I saw that she was here I guessed she'd have brought you along, too, so . . .'

'So you decided to check up on me. Well, here I am, trying to make contact with any spirit who might help me steal your drug.'

He remained unsmiling, but his voice held a hint of amusement as he replied, 'There's no one here who'll help you.'

She began to be vexed as she invariably became in his company. If he were still angry she would have had the advantage and known how to speak to him, but this aloof mockery defeated her.

'However, it won't do any harm for me to keep my eye on you while you stay, just to see that you behave yourself.'

From the light tone of his voice she could not take offence. Involuntarily she found her lips curving into a smile. Despite his levity, though, she was aware of an underlying truth in his words, and it amused her. He really did believe her coming was to find out as much as she could about his discovery, and even when she had gone, empty handed as she must, he would continue to believe it.

He continued to lean easily on the

wall. 'Is this a sentimental pilgrimage, Rowan?' he asked.

'No,' she admitted. 'I came because Laura asked me to, but I'm glad my mother's here and not in some odd corner of Scotland as I'd always believed her to be. I may as well admit that beyond that I feel very little.'

'At least you're honest about that. You don't pretend to feel what it's obvious you don't feel. Why not be honest about the real reason for your visit to Skelvingsdale? I promise I'll forgive you and we can all relax for the rest of your stay.'

She smiled complacently. 'I am relaxed. Very much so. And I have told you the truth.'

She held his gaze steadily and at last it was he who looked away, but there was no perceptible change in his manner as he straightened up and said, 'Here comes Laura. Hello, Laura. Well, I must get along. I have to see about an extension to the drinks licence for Friday.'

He waved cheerily and as Rowan watched him go back to his car it was with mixed emotions; irritation, fascination and a little distrust.

At last, having fixed himself up with a vehicle, there was nothing else for Chris to do, the day before the dance, but to accompany Rowan down the hill. Rowan, herself, while glad of the practical help in carrying down the equipment, was not very glad of his company. In the few days that had passed since the incidents, first with the horse, and then at the churchyard, she had found, alarmingly, that she missed Damon's company. She wanted to be alone, to examine every word that they had exchanged on those occasions, and to consider every expression she had seen cross his face, for it occurred to her that if she were anyone other than Louis Patrick's daughter he would not be so indifferent to her.

She set about the finishing touches to the painting, which had turned out to be quite good, although the moody effect it revealed was not as she had originally planned. Chris sat as she worked and Hamish tore to and fro, chasing birds and insects and barking at his own reflection in the water.

'I'm coming up to London to see you soon,' Chris announced after a while, startling her out of her thoughts.

'I have very little free time, Chris,' she answered; her mind was almost fully on the painting.

'But not all the time.'

'No, but Tony wouldn't be pleased if I spent my spare time with you, and it might be a little awkward for all of us if all three went out together — more than just once, that is.'

Chris tugged at a blade of bracken. On the lower slopes of the distant fells sheep cropped the grass, and growing lambs frollicked until their mothers herded them back to safety.

'I hope this new car of yours is fit for me to go in,' she said lightly a few moments later after noticing his moody expression. 'I don't want to have to summon up my fairy godmother at the last minute. Something tells me pumpkins might not be easy to find in your kitchen.'

To her relief he laughed, although it was a half-hearted effort. 'You don't have to worry; it's not a Rolls-Royce, but it should make a few people around here take notice.'

She looked at him for a long moment as he pulled at the grass, and then said, 'You're nothing like Damon, are you?'

'I'm told I'm like my mother. She was something of a tearaway, too.'

Rowan laid down her brushes and went to sit by his side. Chris drew out a bottle of lemonade while she held the two paper cups for him to pour it into.

As he screwed the top back on to the bottle she said, 'You're not a tearaway, Chris; you only like people to think that you are.'

'And why would that be?' he asked, watching Hamish who was seeking out a rabbit warren.

'I'm not sure I know you well enough

to say. At a guess I think that, even though you could have a career of your own because you're very intelligent, you're afraid of not being able to equal Damon's achievements, so you go in the opposite direction and don't even try to do anything.'

Chris applauded her solemnly. 'Well done. I had no idea that psychology was taught at art school these days.'

She gave him a playful push. 'I don't need to be a psychologist, Chris. You stay at home with your family. If you were the tearaway you'd have us believe you were, you would be away in London all the time, or somewhere equally as lively. You love the countryside. I can tell that much, and you're fond of your home. Tearaways aren't like that. I've met quite a few.

'Perhaps I'm wrong — I probably am — but I'm willing to bet you'll be married and have a respectable crop of children long before Damon will.'

He eyed her steadily. 'Well, that all depends, doesn't it?'

Anxious to keep the conversation light, Rowan got to her feet and brushed the grass off her pants. 'I'm spoken for.'

'So are most girls, I find.'

She laughed. 'You're not going to make me believe you haven't a score to choose from, Chris. Your manner is too well-practised. You only find me interesting because I already have a boyfriend.'

He grinned and jumped to his feet. 'It's getting late. Have you much more to do?'

'No, not very much. You don't have to stay and watch me if you'd rather go, Chris.'

He whistled for Hamish, who came bounding up. 'I'll take the bag and all this other stuff,' he told her, 'and all you have to carry is the canvas and the paints.'

Hamish bounded ahead, up the path, and Chris started to follow. Suddenly he turned and gazed at Rowan for a long moment. 'You can pretend to be detached about us, Rowan, but you have to admit that I haven't impressed you half as much as Damon.'

She stared at him. 'What *do* you mean?'

He grinned maddeningly and, without answering, set off up the path.

Rowan stared after him and then sank down on to the turf. She gazed unseeingly at a clump of blue gentians growing at her side and began to laugh out loud at the realisation that Chris had been perfectly right.

* * *

'There's a telephone call for you, Miss Patrick.'

Rowan stopped as she entered the hall. She looked at Mary who was holding the telephone receiver out to her.

'A telephone call for me?' she echoed.

'Yes, Miss. It's the second this afternoon. Long distance, it is. *Person to person.*'

Rowan handed the girl the canvas. She was slightly winded from her climb and now she was rendered even more breathless by apprehension.

'Mary, will you take this to my room, please? I don't want Mrs Kingsley to see it until it's quite finished. And,' she added as she picked up the receiver from the table, 'take care; some of the paint is still wet.'

'Ain't you clever,' the girl murmured as she took the painting, but Rowan was not listening.

'Rowan Patrick speaking,' she said into the phone. Visions of her father's body floating amidst wreckage in the Aegean crossed her mind.

'Just one moment,' a voice said, and a further second ticked anxiously away. 'You're through now.'

'Rowan? Thank goodness I've found you at last.'

It was Tony's voice and some of her tension drained away. He sounded not at all like the man she was going to marry. He sounded almost a stranger.

'Yes, Tony, what is it?'

'I've been trying to reach you all afternoon. Where have you been?'

'Out. Is there something wrong?'

'Of course there is,' he answered irritably. 'I've been worried about you. You've been gone almost a week.'

Rowan found her own irritation mounting now. 'I didn't say when I'd be back.'

'You said you'd be gone a couple of days.'

'A misjudgement. I decided to give myself a holiday.'

'Just now? Look, Rowan, the real reason I rang up was to ask you to be back tomorrow.'

'Tomorrow? Oh, that's impossible, Tony. I have this dance to go to tomorrow night.'

'A dance!' His voice grew so loud that she had to hold the receiver away from her ear. 'What dance? What on earth are you on about?'

'I can't explain on the phone, Tony. I'll be back on Sunday and I'll tell you

188

all about it then.'

'I don't want to know about it at all, Rowan. What I want is for you to be back in London by tomorrow night. You've had long enough to inspect these long-lost relatives of yours.'

Her lips narrowed into a stubborn line. 'They're not relatives and I'm not coming back until Sunday. I've promised Chris Halstead I'll go — oh, and I *want* to go. I've bought a new dress specially.'

She knew she was being pettish, but as he spoke she could almost see him scowling into the receiver and her resolve hardened. She wasn't used to being dictated to and she wasn't going to start now. It could lead to a great deal of trouble later on.

'You must have taken leave of your senses. I've been asking some questions, Rowan. Did you know that there was a prolonged court case?'

'Yes,' she answered wearily. 'I've heard all about it.'

'You were the centre of a custody

battle and your father sued Halstead for enticement. There was a scandal that would make even today's blasé reporters blush.'

'You sound like one yourself. I didn't think you were so easily shocked.'

'I'm beginning to wonder if I'm speaking to the right person. Are you sure you're aware of the facts?'

'Perfectly sure, but it was twenty years ago, Tony, and both my mother and Mr Halstead are now dead. The matter is not as simple as it seems and I've no intention of discussing it on the phone with you.'

'I don't think you should stay there, Rowan. You owe some loyalty to your father, not to mention your loyalty to me. I don't know what nonsense they've filled you with, but I know your father wouldn't want you to be there.'

'Perhaps not, but I don't have to have Daddy's permission.'

'Look, Rowan, I'm trying to be reasonable. I don't care what you've promised this person, but I happen to be your fiancé and I want . . . '

'You're not my fiancé. We're not engaged yet.'

His sigh carried easily over the miles. 'That's only a formality. If you hadn't gone haring up there you'd have had the ring on your finger right this minute. Let me explain, Rowan, and I'm sure you'll realise how important your immediate return is.'

'Explain away,' she invited coldly.

'I told my boss I was planning to get married in the near future and he was delighted. He likes his men to be married. Most firms do. Well, he wants us to have dinner with him and his wife tomorrow night. When I accepted I thought you would be back days ago. It's as well I have a good memory and could remember where you'd gone. So now you know. Be a good girl now, pack your things, and set off first thing tomorrow.'

'I've already told you — I can't. Tell Mr Anderson we can make it any night next week. It can't be all that important to have me rush back now. I thought something terrible might have happened.'

'Rowan! Will you listen to me! You just won't make the effort to understand. This *is* important. It might mean an early promotion — a partnership, and I don't have to explain what that would mean in terms of money and prestige. It's our *future*.'

'I don't think much to our future, Tony, if we have to jump every time Mr Anderson cracks the whip.'

There was a momentary silence and then he said quietly, 'If that's the way you feel, Rowan, perhaps we'd better not bother at all. A man needs a wife who will support him in his work and not put her own selfish pleasures first.

'It's something I'd always looked for in you. You always made an excellent hostess for your father and, above all, I believed your loyalty above question.'

'Tony, this is a most ridiculous conversation. I can't believe it's taking place. You sound just like an old bore.

When I considered our future, it wasn't as a toady to your business acquaintances. That is something I've never had to do for my father.'

'I'll tell you something, Rowan,' he answered heatedly. It startled her, for she had rarely seen him even mildly annoyed. 'Mother always said your father had brought you up too indulgently; that you'd be too selfish to be the type of wife any hardworking man needs.'

'Oh, for heaven's sake, Tony! Let's not bring your mother into the conversation. She was glad enough to welcome me *because* of my father — and his money, so she'll have to put up with the rest of me. I'm not coming tomorrow, and that's final.'

She slammed down the receiver and took a great gulp of air. What on earth have I done? she asked herself. She was aghast at her own actions.

A sound behind her made her whirl round. With one arm negligently on the newel post, Damon was standing in the shadow of the staircase.

'Do you usually listen in to private conversations?' she asked, fighting back her tears.

'This hall is not the place in which to hold a private conversation. You should have used the phone in the study.'

'I didn't know there was one.' She blew her nose noisily.

She was forced to pass him to go up the stairs. When she drew level he said, in the manner of a man who had just enjoyed what he had heard, 'Chris isn't worth what you've just done.'

'I didn't do it for Chris,' she answered, and her spirits rallied.

'Well, I've no doubt someone of your charms will soon replace him. I bet you have his successor in mind right now.'

She clenched her handkerchief into a ball in her fist. 'You will persist in believing I'm some kind of Mata Hari, won't you?'

'I'm not so bigoted that I can't be persuaded otherwise.'

She stared at him, unable to think of

a reply, until the door opened and Hamish came bounding in. He rushed straight up to Damon who tussled with him roughly until Chris came in, and then the animal bounded back.

Damon brushed a few of Hamish's hairs from the sleeve of his jacket. He glanced at Rowan and then at his brother, and there was a malicious glint in his eye.

'Good news for you, Chris,' he said, to Rowan's fury. 'Rowan has just broken off her engagement — for you.'

Leaving Rowan furious and Chris to digest this surprise piece of news, Damon walked calmly into the study and closed the door.

* * *

'It's too fine an evening to stay in,' said Chris, coming away from the window. He put down his coffee cup and looked at Rowan. 'Come with me to The Duck and Gun. We can sit by the lake and have a drink. It's very pleasant there and it will be something else you can remember me for when you've gone back to London.'

Rowan shook her head. She knew he wanted to question her. That was precisely the reason she had avoided his sole company since the phone call. The last thing she wanted to be right now was sociable. That she was able to dismiss Tony, whom she had hoped to marry, so easily astounded her. Only a week ago she had been delighted to think of a possible marriage.

She wished she could go to her room to examine her thoughts more deeply. The memory of the telephone call still rankled, even more so when she began to understand that the most upsetting part was that Damon had overheard and misconstrued what had been said.

Damon hadn't stayed for dinner, and the house seemed empty and spiritless without him. She felt as lost and as helpless as a spring lamb that had wandered too far across the fells and had tumbled into a ravine from which there was no escape. How she had managed to fall in love with Damon Halstead she would never know, but from the way her heart beat faster whenever he was near her, and the desolation she experienced whenever she knew he was with Carolyne Griffin, it must be so. Ironically she might never have realised it if Chris hadn't practically pointed it out to her that very afternoon.

Laura peered at her; there was a worried frown marring her face. 'Don't think you're being polite by staying with us, Rowan. Go with Chris if you want to. You may as well make the most of your time here.'

Rowan decided that there was no point in brooding over something she could not help. If she couldn't be with Damon — even arguing with him — she may as well keep Chris company.

'You look nice,' he said as they went out of the house, and she was surprised at the sincerity in his voice. 'When you wear jeans you look just like a kid, but when you wear a dress like that, you look quite a woman.'

She laughed. 'Which do you prefer?'

'A little of both.'

She handed him the car keys. 'That phone call really upset you, didn't it?' he said as they set off. The car hood was down and a glorious breeze ruffled her hair. She put her head back on the seat.

'I'll get over it, I suppose.'

'Is it true you had an argument over me?'

'Can't you tell when Damon's joking? He's got an odd sense of humour. We had an argument, Chris. We'll make it up when I get back,' she added, but there was no real conviction in her voice.

The car park of The Duck and Gun was crowded with cars this evening, but Chris managed to find a small space to squeeze in the Triumph.

'This place is popular for miles around on summer evenings as good as this one,' he explained as he helped her out. 'You can sit outside at the back, overlooking the lake.'

'It's as well,' she answered. 'We'd probably suffocate inside. There's not a breath of air.'

'We needn't go inside at all,' he explained, leading her round the side of the inn. 'This kind of weather always ends up in a ferocious storm in these parts, but with a little bit of luck it won't happen until you've gone.'

'I don't know about luck. I wouldn't mind my visit ending with a big bang.'

They came round the side of the inn. Dozens of tables had been set out in a wide yard leading right up to the water. To Rowan's surprise there was even a small jetty and a boathouse, too. Several boats were out on the lake. Most of the tables had people crushed around them, and a white-jacketed waiter was weaving his way through with a ladened tray held aloft. A crowd of people were at the water's edge where the ducks were jostling together to be fed the titbits being offered.

'I haven't seen the ducks before,' commented Rowan.

'They stay at this end because this is where they get fed. If they relied on the inhabitants of Skelvingsdale Hall they'd die of starvation. Oh, look, there's Jim and Belinda Griffin. We'd better go and say what's necessary.'

'Do we have to?' Rowan asked sharply.

Chris laughed in amazement. 'Why not? They'll be itching to meet you, and we can't snub them, can we?'

Very reluctantly, she allowed Chris to guide her past the tables to where the Griffins were seated. Jim Griffin had a clipped moustache and a hearty manner, and jumped to his feet to greet them. Belinda Griffin was a wide-hipped woman with a very pink complexion and blonde hair that might have been that colour naturally once. She displayed none of her husband's enthusiasm for their company and stared at Rowan in a way that the girl considered to be rude. Rowan recalled

Chris's description of her riding to hounds and felt she would have recognised the woman anywhere.

It was possible that Carolyne would resemble her mother when she reached middle-age, and Rowan wondered if Damon had considered the possibility. If he had, though, would he care? Was marriage just an expedient, his work the only thing that mattered?

'We've heard a lot about you, Miss Patrick,' she said, allowing herself a depreciating smile after ignoring Rowan just long enough for it to be noticeable to the girl only.

'Do sit down and join us,' invited her husband, and before Rowan could protest a chair had been pulled out for her.

For the next few minutes Belinda Griffin addressed Chris exclusively in a bright and forced way that, to Rowan, seemed insincere. It was what she labelled a social voice; so many people she had met used one. When she thought of Laura's quiet sincerity, the

201

difference between her and Belinda Griffin was enormous.

'Having an enjoyable stay?' Jim Griffin asked, rubbing his hands together briskly.

Rowan smiled absently. 'Yes, thank you, lovely.'

Two shadows fell across the table. Rowan looked up sharply and her heart turned over at the sight of Damon and Carolyne. Carolyne looked furious, although there was a tight smile on her face.

As they sat down Carolyne's mother said to no one in particular, 'Carolyne is such a child at times. She will never come here without bringing something for the ducks. She just adores animals.'

Carolyne looked at Rowan. Her eyes contained that same look of malice which had been present on the last occasion they had met.

'I hope you've recovered from your accident,' she said.

'Quite,' Rowan answered shortly.

Belinda Griffin turned her attention

back to Rowan again as if she had only just remembered her presence. She smiled frostily. 'Really, it's a great mistake to ride good horses when one just isn't used to it.'

Rowan flashed her an acid smile. 'I am used to riding good horses — usually thoroughbreds. My father wouldn't allow me to ride less. He always said mixed breeds were more like to be temperamental. Perhaps that was where the trouble lay this time.'

Knowing the woman's addiction to horses, Rowan was sure such a slight on her daughter's animal must touch a raw nerve. She noted with pleasure that it had, and as she looked away she caught Damon's eye and was almost certain he was smiling.

His skin was lightly tanned, highlighted by the white sweater he was wearing. She had never seen him look so casual, nor had she seen Carolyne look so pretty. Out of the jodhpurs and shapeless jumpers she usually wore, she was a very attractive girl.

Belinda Griffin recovered herself quickly and turned to Damon and her daughter, smiling sweetly. 'Didn't you two children intend to take out a boat?'

Carolyne flashed Rowan yet another malice-ladened look and began to get to her feet. 'There was just one boat available. Actually, we only came back to let you know we were taking it out.' She looked at Chris quickly and then away, murmuring, 'You'll have to excuse us.'

'Just a minute,' Damon said in a lazy voice. 'I'm not exerting myself when the local sculling champion is present. Go on, Chris, this is more your mark than mine.'

Carolyne flushed slightly and looked at her shoes. Her mother looked as if she were about to say something, but her husband spoke instead, quickly as he glanced at his watch, 'You can argue the point between you. Lindy and I must be off. Thursday's our bridge night.' Mrs Griffin looked disinclined to go, but her husband got to his feet and

204

decided the matter. 'Come along, my dear, you know how the Hendersons go on if we're so much as five minutes late.'

Mrs Griffin collected her outsize handbag and drew the edges of her cardigan together over her ample bosom. 'Yes, I suppose we must go. Well, enjoy yourselves, whatever you choose to do, only do be careful. One hears of so many tragedies on the lakes at this time of the year.' She beamed at Damon. 'Although I must say Jim and I can always rest content when she is with you, Damon. We know you will take care of our little girl.'

She stopped gushing the moment her eyes alighted on Rowan. 'No doubt we shall meet again tomorrow, Miss Patrick,' she said stiffly.

Rowan gazed at her steadily. 'Oh yes, Mrs Griffin; I shall be there.'

A moment later when they had gone, each having bestowed a fond kiss on the cheek of their 'little girl', Carolyne said in an impatient voice, 'Make up your mind whether you're taking me or not, Damon, otherwise there's no point in keeping the boat reserved. You had no objection to going out when it was suggested earlier.'

Damon simply looked at his brother and raised one eyebrow in query.

'I came with Rowan. Much as I'd love to take Caro on the water, I can hardly . . . '

'I'm quite capable of sitting here until you get back,' Rowan pointed out, wishing she had not come. 'Don't let me stop you, Chris.'

Damon smiled in his most maddening way. 'I shall be here to make sure no one tries to make off with her.'

Rowan felt bound to give him a smile of encouragement and a moment later they were pushing their way through the crowds towards the boathouse.

'I'm sorry, I shouldn't have deprived you of his company.'

His tone couldn't have betrayed less sorrow. He was sitting uncomfortably close, with his arm resting along the back of her chair. Rowan was aware that if she moved one inch further in his direction she could be in his arms.

'I don't mind.'

'Would you like me to order you a drink while we're waiting for them to come back?'

'No, thank you. I only came because Chris wanted to go out. I'm not thirsty. But please don't let me stop you.'

He didn't move away from her, and even though she kept her eyes averted she knew his gaze remained fixed upon her face.

She turned her attention to the view all around. The gorse-covered crags were turned to pure gold in the light of the dying sun. High up on the hill stood Skelvingsdale Hall. The sun was shining on its windows, making the house appear ablaze.

'Awesome, isn't it?' said Damon, and it was as if he could exactly read her thoughts.

'Fantastic.'

'I remember the first time I saw the

sun setting on the house from the lake. I was only a very small child. I ran all the way home crying my eyes out because I thought my home was on fire, and the only thing that bothered me was that my old rocking-horse would be burnt.'

'If the house is ever turned into an hotel I shall be the first guest,' she told him.

'You sound as if you're hoping it will be.'

She laughed. 'Only for my own selfish sake.'

'You'll have to wait until the Halsteads are extinct. There's very little chance that both Chris and myself will remain unmarried.'

A sudden roar made them both turn their attention to the lake. Two youths who had been trying to attract the attention of two girls in another boat had managed to overturn their own. Everyone watched a little breathlessly as they surfaced and there was a spontaneous outburst of applause, and

Rowan applauded the loudest, as they righted the boat and climbed back into it.

'I'm glad to see you're not brooding over your broken engagement,' he said, looking at her again.

Her laughter faded. 'Just because I'm not red-eyed doesn't mean to say I'm not upset.'

'I don't doubt that you are upset. It was a distressing conversation. But being upset is a luke-warm emotion where such a matter is concerned. You don't appear to me to be a luke-warm kind of person. Your mother wasn't, and we all know that your father isn't.'

Rowan stared at him coldly. 'You may have discovered how a trout 'works', Damon, but despite all your many qualifications you know precious little about human emotions.'

'It would be more accurate to say I know little about *female* emotion,' he answered easily. 'I do know that if this man meant anything to you, you wouldn't be here; you'd be half-way to

London by now.'

His eyes were full of amusement. She hated him his complacency. His supposition was far too near the truth for her liking. She was half-afraid that he might even go further and guess she had fallen in love with him.

Fortunately, she was saved the necessity of replying by the arrival of a young married couple of Damon's acquaintance, and Rowan was able to talk to the wife until Chris and Carolyne returned and it was time to go back.

8

The house bore a festive atmosphere the following morning. It seemed that, for Laura, the coming dance was one of the highspots of her year. After having breakfast with the excited woman, Rowan retreated to her room with one of the morning newspapers. Chris had gone out already, to collect his new car. Rowan needed badly to be alone.

The previous evening when she had at last returned from The Duck and Gun with Chris she had been both relieved and disappointed that there were no messages for her, although she really expected none. There was nothing more for either of them to say. Tony was disappointed in her, and Rowan believed he had a right to be. It was obvious now that she hadn't loved him enough, and in dismay she tried to conjure up the feelings that had led her to believe, such a short time before, that she could spend the rest of her life with him.

He had loved her in his fashion too, but now that she had failed this crucial test Rowan knew there would be no second chance, and she was dejected at the thought that love could be so unenduring. And she was disappointed at her own failure to mourn the death of what had been between them. But try as she would, she just could not be sorry it was over between them. Rather, it was something of a relief. She could think about Damon with no feeling of guilt.

When she tried to discover why he held such a fascination in her mind, she was completely puzzled. She knew she should hate him, but when she tried to recall his anger all she could remember was his tenderness.

She was sure she would never again find a man with all the qualities he possessed, just as she knew she had never met anyone with a character so complex before. And when he was married to Carolyne, long after he had forgotten she existed, she would still remember.

When she came down again mid-morning, Laura was just coming into the hall. She had a tall coffee pot in her hand and her face lighted into a smile when she saw Rowan.

'I wondered if you were still in, Rowan. I'm neglecting you terribly. I've relied too much on Chris keeping you company, although I dare say he's a great deal better for you than I am.'

'Don't bother yourself on my behalf, Laura,' Rowan answered. 'Considering that I came without warning you've . . . all been very kind. I realise you lead a very busy social life and I don't mind being on my own sometimes. In fact, I like it.'

'We were just about to have coffee and I'd hoped you'd be around to join us.'

'I'd love to.'

'Good. Would you be a dear and go

and tell Damon it's ready? He's in the study. You might have to knock more than once if he's particularly involved — which he usually is,' she ended with a fond laugh.

'Damon?' Rowan echoed. 'I didn't know he was in.'

'Yes, dear. He's doing some work at home today. Run along, before the coffee gets cold.'

Like a sleepwalker, Rowan turned and went across the hall to the small study which she knew Damon and Robert sometimes used. Only today she was unprepared . . . suddenly her feet were light. With so little time left in which to see him, to be near him, this was an extra bonus she had not expected. This feeling of soaring, this delight in his nearness, was something she had never experienced before and never would again. To feel this way, to be in love, was wonderful, but those emotions could be sublime if that love was returned.

She shivered delightedly at the very

thought of it. Then she forced all personal thoughts from her mind as she knocked on the door.

As Laura had suggested, she had to knock twice, and then, at his rather irritable 'Yes', opened the door.

'Laura asked me to tell you coffee is ready.' Her self-consciousness with him made her stiff and her voice cold. It was her only defence. She would die rather than let him suspect her feelings.

He looked up as she spoke. He'd been poring over some papers that were spread across the desk.

It was a small room with space for little more than the desk and the chair it contained. There was no window open and it was impossibly warm in the room. He was sitting at the desk with his jacket over the back of the chair and his shirt sleeves rolled up. A set of golf clubs stood in the corner.

'May I?' she asked, coming into the room, and opened the window to let in what little air there was.

He smiled sheepishly. 'Thanks.'

Laura was just pouring the coffee when they came in. 'I've time for just one cup and then I must be off for my hairdressing appointment.' She looked at Rowan. 'After that I'm going to the golf club to check on the seating arrangements and to make sure the caterer has his orders clear. Some snags always crop up at the last minute.'

Far from being daunted by this possibility, Laura looked rather pleased at the prospect of doing battle with people who invariably get their orders wrong. Laura, Rowan guessed, was very much the social personality, possibly as an antidote to her natural shyness.

'Surely you don't have to do it all?' Rowan asked. 'You're not even working for the firm.'

'I do very little,' Laura admitted as she gulped down her coffee the moment it was cool enough. 'Most of the arrangements are the same year after year, and they're made by Jim Griffin's secretary from the office, but she has her own work to do as well, so

Belinda and I always supervise the last-minute arrangements at the golf club itself.'

'In the past it was always Delia and I who did it.' Laura smiled across at Damon, who was unusually quiet. 'Belinda gets there first and by the time I arrive she's upset the staff and the caterers so thoroughly I have quite a job undoing all her harm.' She gave Rowan an earnest look. 'Not that Belinda means harm. She's really the soul of goodness, but she's one of these narrow women — not in build of course — ' laughing, 'and she can't see any point of view but her own. One year when I arrived the waitresses had their coats on and were on the point of walking out, and it was left to me to pacify them.'

'Which I'm sure you did,' Rowan added with a smile. 'You two have contradictory natures — or at least it seems so from what I've seen of Mrs Griffin.'

As an afterthought she gave Damon

an apologetic glance when she remembered that Mrs Griffin was probably going to be his mother-in-law, but his face bore no expression of particular interest. They could have been talking about anyone.

'I'll take that as a compliment,' said Laura.

'It was meant to be,' Rowan couldn't help herself adding.

Laura gulped down the last of her coffee and stood up to smooth her skirt. 'It's only to be hoped that Carolyne doesn't grow to be a bulldozer, too.' Without a glance in her brother's direction, she said quickly, 'Well, I must be off now, or I won't be going anywhere this morning. See you later, you two.'

When she had gone Rowan glanced rather selfconsciously at Damon. 'Can I get you some more coffee?'

He was sitting well back in the chair, watching her carefully through half-closed eyes. 'As before.'

Aware that he watched her, her hand

shook slightly. As she handed him the cup she said, in as light a tone as she could manage, 'Have you decided to give yourself a holiday from work today?'

'Hardly.' He sat up and took the cup from her. 'I know of old it's impossible to get any work done today, so I stay at home and do it here. All the girls are able to concentrate on today is the way they're having their hair done or whether the gold shoes or the silver shoes match best. And of course,' he added, smiling in a deprecating way, 'there's the most important business of deciding whether they're going to wear pink beads or blue. I'm best out of the way.'

Rowan could well imagine the excitement at the prospect of all the social barriers tumbling down at the coming dance. Office boys could dance with the boss's secretary and typists flirt with the directors; it was all permitted for this one night.

However, she could also imagine

Damon's irritation at what he would consider a trivial affair compared with the project on which he had worked for so long.

'I'm sure if you exerted enough pressure you could have the dance stopped.'

His eyes opened wide in surprise. 'What makes you think I'd want to do a thing like that? Apart from the fact that we'd have a general strike on our hands, I believe it's a good idea. We're a family firm . . . '

More so when you marry Carolyne, thought Rowan.

'From the time my grandfather founded the company we've always maintained good staff relations, and what better way than this is there?'

'You don't have to convince me. I need very little excuse to celebrate.'

'Oh, and what are you celebrating tonight? The ending of your engagement?'

'I had hoped that wouldn't be mentioned again. If we are to be accurate, I wasn't engaged at all, only about to be. It's still a painful experience. I don't like unpleasantness in any form.'

'You didn't let mine chase you away.'

'Possibly because you intended that it should. I was never one to resist a challenge, either.'

'Ah, the Patrick strain again. It's amazing the way family likenesses are refined and passed on.'

She gave him an acid smile. 'It would be a good basis for research.'

'I agree it would be fascinating, but it's not my field.'

She looked straight at him. 'Damon, I don't think I deserve to be blamed for something I had no part in.'

'I'm not blaming you.' His voice was soft. She kept on looking at him, challenging him to say more. When he put his empty cup down he said, deliberately changing the subject, 'How is it you're not rushing off to the hairdresser like everyone else?'

Instinctively her hands went to her

hair and pulled it back from her face. 'Hairdressers don't do very much for me, unfortunately, so I manage it myself. Oh, I've tried hairdressers, but I always come out feeling as though I've got a cardboard box on my head. Don't worry, I won't disgrace you tonight.'

'That's certain, because you won't be with me. You're going with Chris.'

He was studying her curiously, with a heartbreaking detachment. It was a disconcerting experience, but at least he was interested enough to take time off from his precious work to talk to her. It was as much as she could ever expect from him.

'Didn't your father ever try to make you into a debutante type?'

'There's no presentation at Court these days, so much of the prestige has gone out of being a deb.,' she answered drily. 'Besides, I have no wish to marry into the aristocracy.'

'I imagine your father would like that, though.'

'Any father would. But, yes, I would

be a fool to deny it — he would. He has lots of money and everything that goes with it. It would give him a great deal of satisfaction to see me married into a distinguished line. He's worked for his money; it wasn't inherited.'

'I lead a very satisfactory social life. My father gave up trying to make me give in to his whims years ago. Perhaps we're too much alike for him to have a great deal of influence over me.' She smiled at him. 'There, that admission should confirm your opinion of me.'

'How could you know that when you've no idea what is my opinion of you?'

She gave a mirthless laugh. 'My problem is that I have a very shrewd idea.'

'Have you indeed?' he said, smiling to himself.

She got up, almost overturning her cup and saucer in the process. He caught them for her and set them down on the table. 'I've kept you from your work long enough,' she said without looking at him. 'I'll get along and leave you to go back to it.'

'Where are you going? Don't let me chase you out.'

'You're not. I intended to go for a walk before lunch. I can't get enough of the air out here.'

'The painting is finished, then?'

'All but the finishing touches, which I can easily add tomorrow.'

'I'll walk outside with you. I need a breath of air, too. When I get stuck into a problem I forget all else. Laura always says that the house could easily burn down around me and I'd never know it.'

'It's good to have such concentration,' she murmured. 'The lack of it has always been my problem.'

'Sometimes my concentration is seriously threatened, such as now. I may not get back to it at all today.'

He opened the front door for her and the sunlight flooded in, blinding her for the moment. 'I hope that isn't my fault.'

'You hope no such thing.'

She turned away from the sun, her heart beating so unevenly she marvelled that he did not hear it. She could read nothing in his expression. She wondered what he had meant by his last remark, but somehow couldn't ask.

He stood there, taking in the fresh air and gazing around him, secure in his world. Would he, she wondered, ever give her a thought when she had gone?

'I've a good mind to come with you,' he said only a moment later. 'This weather is too good to miss and the work can wait.'

She looked away, hating the way her blood was leaping at the thought of it. To have him to herself, be it only for an hour, would be marvellous. His attitude towards her had already softened in the few days since she'd arrived; she felt she only needed time before he would trust her completely. That, at least, would be something.

Whether he mistook her hopeful silence for discouragement she was not to know, for at that moment a roar heralded the approach of a small white sports car. The car came to a halt only a few feet from where they were standing.

When Carolyne got out Rowan's spirits plummeted. She'd had a chance, probably her last, to have him to herself. Carolyne Griffin was just about the last person she would wish to see right now.

'I thought I'd find you here,' Carolyne said, bestowing a charming smile on Damon as he opened the car door for her, and completely ignoring Rowan. 'I had some time to spare, so I thought I'd call in. Mummy is tearing about like someone mad, so I thought I'd better clear out of the way for a while. I expect Laura is the same this morning.'

'Laura never tears about. She fusses, but that's her limit.'

Now that there was no chance of him coming with her, Rowan turned away and started down the hill. It gave her some satisfaction to hear Damon add just then, 'But just because I'm at home today, Carolyne, doesn't mean that I have nothing to do. I'm working on something important just now.'

'You always are, but you didn't seem to be doing very much work just now.' Rowan could almost feel Carolyne's malevolent stare on her back. 'Important or not, you had plenty of time for her.'

'I don't think I have to explain my every movement to you, Carolyne,' he told her and his voice was sharp, but then he added with a gentleness that hurt Rowan, 'Go along inside; there's plenty of coffee in the pot. I'll be in in just a second and we can chat for a while.'

Rowan knew that he was following her. It would take him only seconds to catch up with her, yet perversely she kept on walking. He had only suggested going with her; it wasn't very much, yet she felt as if she had been robbed of something momentous.

He came up to her, taking the path in large strides, and caught her arm. 'I'm sorry you had to hear that, Rowan. She doesn't . . . '

Rowan smiled, but her face was tight. 'You don't have to apologise for her, Damon. I don't need to be told that Miss Griffin dislikes me. That much I can see for myself. It isn't her fault. She believes only what she's been told.'

'Not by me.'

She tossed her hair back from her face. 'Does it matter who told her or why? I won't be here long enough to live down my reputation as Louis Patrick's daughter, and I'm not sure I want to. He has his faults, but he's a marvellous man in so many ways. You're a purist; scientists usually are. You couldn't understand that a businessman needs to be ruthless and that ruthlessness sometimes spills over into private life. What I find hard to take is that you assume that I would be the same.

'I don't envy my mother's task in living down her reputation in this place if everyone is like you, but, then, she lived here for twenty years which might just have been enough. In a couple of days I shall be gone and you can spend the rest of your life being proud of having stopped my wicked schemes.'

She pulled away from him and plunged down the path. He made no move to follow her, but she knew he was watching, and maddeningly her eyes blurred with tears.

*　*　*

She came down the staircase slowly, the soft folds of her dress brushing her ankles. She had swept her hair high on top of her head; her neck and shoulders were unadorned, but for the first time she wore her mother's emerald-and-diamond ring. It held no unhappy memories for her. On the contrary, it had been given at a very happy time, when her mother and father had been very much in love. She wondered how long it had taken for that love to die. She didn't doubt that it was her father's preoccupation with his own pursuits that had been its prime cause. A gentle, home-loving woman would have hated the life Louis Patrick would force her to lead, and business would always come first. Men like my father should never marry, she thought. Tony was ambitious, too; he would always give business priority over wife and family, she realised at last, and she was glad of her escape. She wondered why she hadn't realised it earlier, for she had always considered Tony to be like her father.

Inevitably her thoughts turned to Damon. He was devoted to his work, too, but not solely in order to make money. Perhaps, if there was love in his life, he would spend less time at his work, especially now that the project was nearing a successful conclusion. No man could expect to pioneer more than one major scientific discovery.

Perhaps . . . Rowan smiled to herself . . . It was a nice thought.

Dreams were all very well, but he

would drift into a marriage with Carolyne. He was fond of the girl, certainly, but it would bring him only social and business prestige, not the overwhelming love she had for him. Rowan wondered if her own love for him would die in time, as her mother's love had died of starvation when there had been nothing for it to feed upon. Rowan felt she might meet someone else too, fall in love again surely. But was a second love ever as breathless and wonderful and agonising as the first?

A long, low wolf-whistle greeted her as she came down the stairs. 'Wow! You look fantastic!' exclaimed Chris when he saw her.

In his dinner jacket, with his unruly fair hair for once tidy, he looked quite handsome himself. She need not be ashamed of her partner, only it was Damon's company she craved. She could have laughed at the perversity of life.

Laura and Robert had left only minutes ago, but Rowan knew that

Damon had gone some time before — to collect Carolyne, she was sure.

She linked her arm into Chris's. 'You look something yourself, Chris, and however many girls you take out in the future I shall have the distinction of being the first to ride in your new car. Is the golf club very far?'

'Not nearly far enough. We're going to arrive far too soon when, just now, I feel like keeping you to myself.'

★ ★ ★

The dinner was over, a surprisingly good one, too. Rowan was relaxed, having been fortified by two aperitifs and several glasses of dinner wine. The company at the table to which they had been assigned was pleasant, but it didn't stop her looking constantly to the table at the top of the room where Damon was sitting. Next to him was Carolyne. It had come as something of a shock for Rowan to see how glamorous and vivacious Carolyne looked. With her hair set into a soft style and a dress that was far more fetching than her usual jodhpurs and sweater, she was a girl with whom any man could be proud of being. Rowan frequently caught sight of Damon bending his head to hers as she spoke, or with his arm negligently around her shoulders. Rowan felt quite sickened by her own jealousy of such innocent actions.

As for Damon himself . . . she had never considered him handsome, but the dark dinner jacket against the white of his shirt became his dark looks so well that every time she looked at him it brought a lump to her throat. In his turn he hadn't even glanced at her since she had arrived, but from her smiling performance during the evening no one could possibly guess the hurt that he had caused.

As with most inept speakers, Jim Griffin's speech had been a long one. Now it was over and many people were thankfully moving about, some to the bar to fortify themselves for the dancing, and others to seek an elusive breath of fresh air.

Chris led her away from the crowds towards the fire escape. 'Just what I need,' she said when a cool gust of air met them as he pulled open the door.

No one else had come out this way. Rowan walked over to the iron railings and looked down to where crowds of people were standing below.

'It's cooler up here,' she said at last, aware that Chris was watching her.

'I wanted to get you on your own, and no one ever comes out this way. I don't know why. And I don't know why it is, but you're elusive to me, Rowan, even when we're together.'

She turned to smile at him. 'What is it you want? A loan, or are you wanting to tell me your darkest secret?'

He pulled her close to him. 'I want this,' he said as he began to kiss her. It wasn't an unpleasant sensation. Damon's indifference hurt her pride and this was something of a salve. Guiltily she pushed him away after a few moments. 'Don't spoil it, Chris,' she said breathlessly. 'We've had fun together so far.'

He released her immediately. 'Sorry,' he said cheekily. 'I couldn't resist it. Let's go back to the safety of crowds; the music's started.'

He held open the door for her and just as she was about to pass through she glanced downwards; amongst the people taking the air Damon and Carolyne were standing. Both of them were looking up and it was clear that if they'd been there seconds before they must have seen everything.

Rowan had little time to brood on how Damon might construe that scene, for whenever one dance was finished she was claimed for another, so much so that eventually Chris took her to the bar where, he said, if he had to share her with others he could enjoy her company, too.

As she'd danced with her various partners Rowan had been aware that Damon hadn't been idle either. He had danced not only with Carolyne and Laura, but with many other women, too. He had danced with nearly everyone he knew except for her, and even though she had not been idle herself for one dance since the music began, perversely she was stung by his snub. She was sure everyone else would notice that he was avoiding her. Steady, she warned herself; Damon wasn't even doing her the honour of avoiding her; it was simply that she meant nothing to him. The contentment of his staff would surely be of greater importance than one dance with her; something that would soar her up to the heights of happiness. He hadn't wanted her here and there was no way he could make it more plain.

There were others grouped round the bar and Rowan found herself in the centre of a very interested group who, once they learned where she was from, plied her with questions. Did she know of this club, that restaurant? It was easy to relax and bask in such constant attention and to forget the misery in her heart. She laughed a lot and automatically accepted the drinks as they were offered to her.

As the time passed she began to realise that she had drunk far more than her normal quota of alcohol, but the effect was a pleasant one so she didn't care that her happiness was the bottled kind. Even when Carolyne appeared at her side quite late on in the evening it didn't have the daunting effect her presence usually had.

'Enjoying yourself?' she asked, her smile tight.

'Very much indeed,' Rowan found herself saying in a hearty way that was quite unlike her usual manner.

Carolyne's smile did not waver. 'I am pleased to hear that,' she answered, her manner that of the gracious hostess, 'although I'm surprised you have. I mean, unlike all of us, you have no real connection with Halstead and Griffin.'

Rowan felt like slapping her face and wiping that satisfied smile off her lips.

She had every reason to feel glad. She wondered if Damon had proposed at last, for Carolyne seemed particularly buoyant.

Before Rowan had a chance to think of a quick reply Carolyne had turned to Chris and, in a coquettish way that was completely out of character, said, 'Isn't it time you and I had a dance, Chris? You usually manage to spare me one, whoever you happen to bring along each year.'

Chris slid from his stool and smiled apologetically at Rowan. 'I'll be back soon; don't go away.'

'I'm not going anywhere,' she answered lazily, ignoring Carolyne's parting shot.

As they went she turned away, twirling the cherry round and round in her drink. She wished she hadn't let Chris persuade her to stay for this dance. Every moment of it was humiliating. She should have been away from here days ago. If she had gone as she had planned to do, she would have been back in London getting engaged to Tony instead of pining after a man who despised her.

'Perhaps now I'll have a chance to claim you before someone else does.'

Her head came up sharply at the sound of his voice. 'I didn't see you there, Damon.'

'That's not so surprising; it's very difficult to penetrate your circle of admirers.'

He took her hand in his and held it firmly. Carolyne, in maliciously depriving her of Chris's company, had inadvertently given her all she wanted this evening — the chance to be in Damon's arms.

The tempo was slow and dreamy; several couples had left already and it was getting late.

'Aspiring Mata Haris don't dance yards from their partners,' he said after a moment or two.

At any time she would have been happy of an excuse to be in his arms, but experienced through a mild alcoholic haze it was sublime. She allowed him to draw her close. At best the atmosphere was stifling; now she could hardly breathe.

She laid her cheek against his. 'I know better than to try my charms on you. You know what I'm up to, but I have been trying to find a member of your team who's more susceptible.'

'And . . . ?' He held her away momentarily.

'And,' she answered with a sigh, 'I found that almost all of them are women.'

'I should have thought you would appreciate that, being a career woman yourself. Some of the best scientific brains belong to women.'

'That doesn't help my . . . er . . . assignment? Yes, that's what it is, isn't it? An assignment. Anyway, it's late, and in dinner jackets the lab. technicians look very much like the caretaker or the managing director.'

'Hey, just be careful what you say. Jim Griffin won't take kindly to being likened to the caretaker.'

'I don't suppose he would make a very good lab. technician either. And,' she added, 'I don't think I would make a very good spy.'

He drew her close again. 'In the tradition of all the best spies, you're looking very lovely tonight,' he said softly in her ear. 'You make every other woman in the room look dowdy.'

'There's no reason why I should; I bought the dress locally.'

'I wasn't admiring your dress particularly.'

She stiffened slightly and then relaxed again. She wasn't a child to be taken in by a few words of flattery. It meant little . . . nothing. She mustn't make the mistake of taking him seriously.

'You look very handsome yourself tonight, Damon,' she said in an effort to be lighthearted. 'It's amazing what a dinner jacket does for a man. It's the same thing a black nightie does for a woman.' She pulled away from him, pressing one hand to her lips to stifle a giggle. 'Oh, heavens, I think I'm drunk.'

'Yes, I believe you are,' he agreed, laughing, 'and that's another thing beautiful spies never allow to happen. You should learn to pour it into the potted palm while you ply your victim with alcohol to loosen his tongue.'

'I couldn't find a palm anywhere.'

He took her arm. 'We'd be better employed sobering you up. Come along, we can't stand in the middle of the dance floor indefinitely.'

He led her back towards the bar. 'You're not going to ply me with strong, black coffee, are you?' she asked apprehensively.

'Nothing so ineffectual. I have a much better concoction. The barman will make it up for me.'

She pulled up sharply. 'Really?'

He looked down at her. She was only slightly intoxicated but not so far gone as to throw herself into his arms as she wished to do right at that moment. 'It works. You'll see.'

'Why on earth don't you put it on the

market instead of wasting your time on this other thing? You'd make a fortune.'

'Because 'this other thing' will save millions of lives eventually. And as a matter of interest, this little concoction isn't my invention; it belongs to a friend of mine and he allows it to be used only for friends. If it was marketed, can you imagine the uproar? All the pleasure would be taken out of drinking.'

She laughed as he eased her on to one of the bar stools and gave the barman precise instructions. A minute later Damon was putting the glass into her hand. She looked at it suspiciously. 'Drink up now,' he ordered in a brisk voice.

'I don't know whether I trust you.'

'You won't wake up in my bed, I promise you.'

She coloured up slightly when she thought that she wouldn't mind at all, but told herself it was the heat of the atmosphere and all the drink she had consumed that was the cause of it.

'It's not like you to be so faint-hearted. Drink up.'

She drank it down in one gulp and shuddered. 'I don't know whether it does any good,' she gasped, 'but it certainly puts one off drinking in the future.'

'That's the idea. A double-edged cure. It's not so bad. We used to make gallons of it in specimen jars when I was at university.'

Rowan gave a hoot of laughter. 'I shudder to think what you must have taken by mistake on many occasions.'

'That's a matter for speculation.'

Rowan felt as if she was sparkling. He had that effect on her; it surely couldn't be just the drink. When she recalled a typical conversation with Tony she remembered how serious he always was, and he discussed everything in detail — mostly his work. She would never have believed Damon could be so lighthearted about his.

'What are the ingredients of this thing? I know so many people who'd welcome something to make them sober. With the formula in my handbag I'd be the hit of any party.'

He shook his head and smiled at her. 'You've already been warned — no secret formulas; not even this one.'

She studied him for a moment. 'This isn't the first time you've had to come to my rescue.'

He looked blank for a moment and then smiled when he remembered. She was hurt that he should have forgotten so soon. Every moment she had spent in his company was indelibly etched in her mind.

'So it is. Knight-errantry is becoming quite a habit. I shall have to take it up as a hobby.'

He glanced around at the small, square room and the five-piece band on a dais only just big enough to take it. 'This isn't quite your usual scene, is it, Rowan?'

'I really don't know what you'd consider my usual scene to be, Damon,' she answered lightly.

245

'Large West End hotels, ten-course meals, and ladies in furs — not our homely little gathering.'

Her eyes narrowed. Whatever he had put into that drink was working. Her little world was no longer ringed with a rosy glow.

'Mrs Griffin has a very nice fur, I noticed,' she retorted. 'In fact, she looks rather like a grizzly bear in it.'

Unrepentant about that piece of spitefulness (she reckoned she owed it to Mrs Griffin, who had pointedly ignored her all evening), she was surprised at Damon's answering laugh. 'She does, doesn't she?'

Rowan eyed him mischievously. 'She's also wearing a king's ransom in jewellery.'

'That's something that can't be said about you.'

Obviously he didn't remember making that remark either. 'But it has been said.'

He frowned for a moment and then smiled sheepishly. 'I can't imagine why.'

'Well, wonder of wonders!' Chris

exclaimed as he came up to them. 'You're still where I left you.'

From her facial expression no one could tell how disappointed Rowan was at Chris's return. 'I'm not,' she answered lightly. 'Damon and I have been dancing. Didn't you see us?'

'No,' he answered slowly. 'Caro decided that she'd rather have some fresh air.' He glanced at his brother. 'Thanks for keeping Rowan company. I'll take over now. Carolyne's looking for you.'

After Damon had gone to find Carolyne there was no enjoyment left for Rowan. Ungraciously she wished Chris hadn't come back so soon, although she realised he had, in fact, been gone some time. When he suggested that they leave a few minutes later she was glad to agree. Damon was busy saying goodbye to those who were leaving; he wouldn't speak to her again.

9

The winding road unfolded like a black ribbon in front of them. Rowan snuggled down into the seat as Chris's new car ate up the miles. She didn't feel the slightest bit sleepy; whatever was in Damon's drink had banished sleep completely.

Chris took one hand off the wheel to stifle a yawn and then glanced at her apologetically. 'How is it you're as fresh as when you set out?'

'I rather think I owe it to a concoction Damon made me drink while you were with Carolyne.'

Chris let out a shout of laughter. 'I've had that remedy forced down my throat on more than one occasion. That's why I have such temperate habits these days.'

There was a pleasant silence for a moment or two before Chris smiled to himself and said, 'I believe Carolyne is jealous of you, Rowan.'

She studied him carefully for a moment. Carolyne was always an awkward subject. Then she looked out at the road again. 'I know.'

He glanced at her, his face a picture of surprise. 'You're a cool one.'

'Well, what did you expect me to say? Simper and blush and say, 'Oh, get on with you do'?'

Chris shook his head and laughed. 'I should expect anything from you; you're quite an unusual girl.'

'What is there between you two, and don't say 'Nothing' because there very definitely is.'

Chris drew a small sigh and eased his foot off the accelerator. 'Once, perhaps, but no more. We grew up together. We have a lot of interests in common. We started the riding school together and at one time I thought there might be more . . . '

'But Damon came along.'

'No, that didn't happen until later,

and then so gradually no one really realised they'd paired off. No, it was her mother — at least, I think it was. Carolyne was quite young; she was easy to pressure. For Mrs Griffin her daughter's wedding won't be just a matter of Caro's happiness, it will have to be another step up the social ladder. She knows only too well what work Damon is doing and if he's successful it won't be just a matter of money; it will be fame, too, and public honour.'

Rowan could not dispute his words; she knew they were very likely true. Her own father would, no doubt, be furious if she, herself, decided to marry a man with only a small income, no social status, and few prospects. It was something that occurred in most families at some time or other, but which invariably caused heartache to all those involved.

'It may be no consolation to you, Chris, but I believe she still cares for you.'

'*What?*' The car slowed almost to a standstill. A car which had been following them switched its lights to full beam and roared past.

'Keep your mind on your driving, Chris, please,' she told him, and then, when they were safely on their way again, he said, 'What gave you a crazy notion like that? Why shouldn't she prefer Damon? She might share her mother's liking for the glory to come.'

'She wouldn't be human if she didn't, but few women can be so cold-blooded as to say, 'I'm going to marry that man because he's rich' or for whatever it is she wants. If it were the case, I'd have married a tycoon long ago. There's a little matter of love, which happens to be important, too; and even if Carolyne has been persuaded she loves Damon, I still think she's more fond of you.'

'I wish I could believe you. I've never really managed to get that girl out of my system. No one knows her as well as I do. Everyone thinks she's horsy and animal mad, but there's more to her than that.'

'Everyone's character has many facets, Chris. You said before that Carolyne was jealous of me, and I agreed. Have you considered why she should be? She owes me no personal animosity and Damon hasn't exactly enthused over me. So why should she be jealous? Because you've been at my side almost constantly since I arrived in Skelvingsdale.'

'Very well thought out.' The car came to a halt in front of the house. He sat back in the seat. 'But that explanation is too simple. Every woman present tonight was jealous of you.'

'Perhaps, but I'm convinced that's the core of the matter where Carolyne is concerned. You can dismiss it if you like, but why not, if you *really* care, give her a chance again?'

'Too late,' he said flippantly.

'If you say so, but it seems a pity for you to go through the rest of your life acting the gay playboy just because you couldn't be bothered to try and win at something. Love doesn't just come to those with brains and ability, Chris; it's something common to us all.'

'I don't know, Rowan. I just don't know. I'm not even sure I still want her.'

'If you think about it you probably do. Why else would you stay around here when you could go anywhere you wished? You have a private income and no job to tie you down.'

He took her hand. 'You seem extraordinarily anxious to make a match between me and Caro. Are you sure you don't just want to revenge yourself on Damon for his treatment of you when you arrived?'

She pulled her hand away from his. 'Damon has his work. Somehow I don't think he would waste his time breaking his heart over any woman. May we go in now?'

'You may; I have to put the car away. Will you wait for me?'

'It's late,' she answered. 'I think I shall go straight up.'

He leaned across and kissed her on the cheek. 'Thanks, Rowan.' She knew what he meant. 'I wish it were you and

I; it would be so much simpler.'

Rowan would be the first to admit that it would. Chris Halstead was good-looking and a pleasant companion. It would be simpler if she had fallen in love with him, and also more logical, but emotions were not subject to logic. Chris was in love with Carolyne and Rowan was in love with Damon; facts that no amount of wishing could alter.

She had just gone into the house when another car swept up the driveway, bathing the hall in light for a moment. Rowan hesitated; she heard the slam of a car door and Laura's voice saying, 'Where's Rowan?'

'Gone straight to bed,' answered Chris. 'She must be all in, poor kid.'

Rowan smiled to herself. Sleep was never further away, yet she was not inclined to see Laura just then. Laura, she was sure, would insist on discussing the dance in depth and Rowan had too much on her mind just then. So she slipped quietly into the darkened sittingroom and closed the door. A moment later she heard them all troop through the hall, laughing as they went up the stairs.

When the sound of their voices faded, Rowan relaxed again. She drew her coat from her shoulders and let it slip to the floor. She went across to the window. The room was gently bathed in the glow of the full moon which was suspended over the tarn. She caught her breath at the loveliness of it all. All this, and Damon, too.

She knew he would be home late. He would not leave until the last guest had gone, and then he would take Carolyne home. Rowan wondered what Chris would say if he knew *she* was jealous of Carolyne. Her hands clenched into tight fists at her sides. Her jealousy was as fierce as her love; it was like a fire rampant inside her.

She stiffened as she heard the approach of what she knew must be his car. She hardly dared to draw breath when he entered the hall, and actually held it when his footsteps came nearer.

The door opened. The room was flooded with light. They both blinked; he checked in surprise and then smiled wryly. 'Doing a little haunting by moonlight?'

'Just not sleepy,' she answered in a remarkably even voice as she turned away again.

'Late nights have that effect on me, too.' He came across the room and as he removed the stopper from one of the decanters he asked, 'Join me?'

She laughed and shook her head. 'I've had more than enough tonight, and that concoction of yours has really livened me up.'

He glanced across at her as he stoppered the decanter. 'I suppose you think because of that I should be making cocoa for you.'

'You've made enough drinks for me for one night.' She retrieved her coat from where it lay on the floor. 'I'd better go up now.'

'No, don't,' he said, to her surprise,

as he sat down on the sofa. He patted the space next to him. 'Keep me company for a while.'

She hesitated but knew already that she hadn't the strength of will to refuse such a tempting invitation.

'You're leaving on Sunday, Laura tells me.'

'That should relieve your mind considerably,' she answered without looking at him.

'You really don't have a good opinion of me, even though you hardly know me. Come to think of it, I don't know much about you.'

'You know who's daughter I am, and that seems to be enough for you.'

His ease discomfited her as much as his very presence. He was so unlike the angry man she had seen for the first time only days ago.

'It should be enough for most women, but for you it isn't. By some miracle you've managed to emerge as a person in your own right. I would never have believed it possible, but you are.'

'You wouldn't, by any chance,' she asked in some amazement, 'be complimenting me?'

His eyes, brimming with laughter, looked into hers. 'That's precisely what I am doing.'

'You'll have to excuse my surprise.'

He went over to refill his glass. 'Was she very unhappy about it all, Damon?' she asked.

He didn't answer immediately. He came back with his glass and sat down again, staring at it thoughtfully for a moment. 'Only at first,' he said at last, 'and mostly on our account. But she'd wanted to marry my father too much to be unhappy about something she knew was mostly her own fault. She was happy living here. Occasionally, when it was your birthday, she'd become a little sentimental, which was natural, but she didn't pine. It was your father's determination to do us as much mischief as he could that hurt most of all, I think. She'd loved him once, so I suppose it came as rather a shock that he should try to hurt not only her, but us too, in any way he could find. And he did try, Rowan. My, how he tried.'

She laid her head back wearily. When she had set out from home she had feared she might uncover unpleasant facts; but she had hardly expected to discover this darker side to her father's nature, although, she supposed, she had always known it was there.

'I can understand it in a way, Damon, and, I think, so can you. Daddy isn't a passive man. It comes as a natural reaction for him to hit out hard when he's been hurt. It's an animal instinct I think is in all of us. I think I'd be like that, too. Yes, I'm sure I should. I don't doubt he wasn't an ideal husband — for her anyway — but he did the best he could. He loved her in his way. He hasn't married again and as far as I know he never considered it, which proves he doesn't take marriage lightly.'

'No one has suggested he did.' He put his empty glass down on the floor and turned to her again. 'But he's had his affairs.'

She shrugged. 'What man hasn't? He's free to do so. He always taught me the right moral values and never shirked his responsibility towards me. We shared the apartment until two years ago, and I assure you it wasn't a den of vice.'

As she spoke she realised she would always look upon him differently from now on. He was no longer the colossus who could do no wrong. He was human enough to have failings like any other man. His women friends were legion, yet he was not too strong to lose the one woman to whom he had committed himself completely. Facing the knowledge at last gave her a new awareness and a vulnerability that had not been there before.

She turned, and her face was only inches away from his. 'Why do I bother? What he did to my mother and your family is history. I can't make up for it and I can't excuse it. He believed he was right and so did a court of law, but hasn't it ever occurred to you that I might resent you taking my mother? She gave you a settled childhood, love and companionship.'

'Poor little rich girl,' he murmured drily. 'It must have been a great hardship having everything money could buy, living in luxury and having princesses as schoolmates.'

'You didn't exactly live in poverty.'

'If your father had his way we would. I'm not feeling sorry for you, Rowan.'

'And I'm not looking for your pity,' she answered, sitting up straight. 'I've always been happy, but a nanny and a housekeeper isn't the same as having a mother and a wife. I just want you to realise we lost something, too — and not just a little of the family esteem.'

'So that's how you see me — puffed up with false pride.'

'I didn't say that. Do you still believe my father sent me to ferret out your industrial secrets?'

He threw back his head and laughed

softly. It seemed incredible that she was having this unreal conversation with him in the middle of the night.

'Oh, my dear girl, will you ever forgive me?' He looked at her; her heart beat unevenly whenever he did, even more so now. What was it about the early hours that appealed especially to those in love? 'I wasn't myself that day; haven't you realised it yet? I was taken unawares. I hadn't seen you then — at least, I believed I hadn't — and I hadn't spoken to you.' She said nothing, and he added softly, 'Is my opinion of you so important?'

'Yes, when it was such a bad one. I didn't deserve it, and that rankled. It was a totally unjust condemnation and I hate injustice.'

'I couldn't have a bad opinion of you after tonight.'

She looked up sharply. 'Tonight?'

'You must be aware that there were few men who could keep their eyes off you tonight, especially Chris.'

She felt her cheeks flood with colour

as she recalled him seeing their kiss. He couldn't have possibly known she was an unwilling partner. She turned to face him, an excuse on her lips, but he put his arms around her, saying, 'I've allowed him to monopolise you for long enough. Now it's my turn.'

Her arms slid around his neck. She didn't even care if he were insincere, if this were the result of a pleasant evening or, perhaps, one drink too many. When he kissed her she could believe he cared, and tomorrow could take care of itself.

'I've wanted to do that since I first saw you,' he murmured against her hair.

'I would never have known it,' she answered, sighing happily as he kissed her again.

Blood pounded through her veins, quickening in response to his every kiss.

'It wasn't a simple matter. Not for me. I can't be casual. I had to be sure of so many things first.'

Her arms tightened around him. 'I'm

glad you're not casual, even though it's taken you so long to learn to trust me.'

'Trust and love often come together.'

Rowan hardly dared to believe what he was saying. Here in the intimacy of the night nothing could be believed, and yet she did.

She lost track of time. Morning could come as late as it wished. Whatever tomorrow held in store could not be as delightful as the present.

'What a lovely way to end the day,' she sighed when he released her at last. His hand slid into hers and she stayed very close to him.

'The day ended hours ago. We're well into the new one.'

'Then it's a lovely way to start the day.'

'With many more lovely days to come.'

He kissed her again. He took hold of her other hand and drew her to her feet. Happily she allowed him to lead her up the stairs and when, outside her room, he kissed her again she clung on to him tightly, reluctant to let him go lest he became a stranger to her again.

'Sleep tight,' he whispered as his hold on her loosened. 'We have a lot to talk about in the morning.'

She closed the door and stood with her back against it for a long while.

'*We have a lot to talk about . . .* '

It sounded very much like a promise.

10

Rowan awoke the following morning to the sounds of the house coming awake. One glance at her watch told her it was very late, but she simply turned over and let her mind dwell delightedly on all that had occurred between her and Damon the night before.

They had to talk; there was so much to discuss. What a surprise for Laura and Chris!

She threw back the covers and crossed to the window. It was a beautiful day again, not a leaf or a blade of grass stirred, and the waters of the tarn shone like a mirror reflecting her happiness.

Never before had she experienced this radiance that came from within to enclose her in its glow. She had never been so complete or so contented before. It was as if she had come to the end of a long, long road to find that Utopia lay before her. Living is just existing without love, she thought.

Rowan hoped that they would have an opportunity to be alone; that Damon hadn't gone to the laboratory to work alone while the rest of his staff were recovering from the evening of revelry. She hoped that Chris wouldn't try to monopolise her, or that Laura wouldn't be insensitive to their need to be alone.

Surely, she thought, Damon won't allow that to happen after what had passed between them only hours before. That precious time had been very real and, she was convinced, just the start of true happiness.

They could drive out into the country together to discuss their future. It had to be together, for otherwise there was no future at all.

She skipped eagerly down the stairs. As she passed the study on her way to the breakfast room she almost cannoned into him just as he was coming out. She laughed breathlessly as he steadied her, expecting to be greeted as joyously by him. Then she looked up at him and her laughter died.

'What is it, Damon?' she asked when she saw the expression on his face. 'What has happened?' He looked as he had done the first time they met in this house, and she felt chilled through.

'You bitch!' he cried.

'Damon!'

He pulled her into the room, his hands rough on her arm. His fingers were biting into her flesh, but she was so bewildered and frightened that she hardly noticed. She was almost thrown into the room and would have fallen if she hadn't steadied herself against the desk. Her frightened eyes came to rest on the total confusion all around. The drawers had been pulled out and their contents spilled on top of the desk and on to the floor.

'You actually have the cheek to look innocent and ask me what's happened! I trusted you. I even . . . ' He caught her by the arm and swung her round to face him again. 'Where is it, Rowan? You'd better tell me.'

He raised his hand and she was so sure he was going to hit her that she flinched.

'Damon! What is going on?'

He swung round to face his sister. 'It's gone, Laura. Gone, and I'm trying to get this . . . ' he looked at her with a disgust that made her die inwardly, 'this guest of ours to tell me where she's put it. But she's clever. Much cleverer than any of us believed. I would never have believed her to be so gifted. No one can learn to act so innocently; it has to be natural.'

Rowan looked from one to the other in bewilderment. 'Put what? What is it that's gone?'

'Yes, I should like to know that, too,' Laura said quietly.

'The file I was working on yesterday.' He let go his hold on Rowan as if even the slightest contact with her repelled him and, as his hold on her slackened, some of the fury seemed to drain from him, too. What was left was an unbearable coldness.

'It was a detailed progress report on the test we've done so far. I'd compiled it for the board meeting next week. Now, unless I get it back, I shall have to tell them that I was the victim of the oldest trick in the world — I fell for a woman's charms.'

'Oh, Damon!' she cried. 'I never did it! I had no idea what you were doing yesterday.'

He looked at her scathingly; his lips were pressed into a grim line. It was hard to believe just then that he had been so gentle and loving only hours ago.

'It was a simple matter for you to find out. You only had to read it. You didn't even have to understand it. Whatever it was, there was a good chance that it was something of importance.'

Laura came right into the room. She had been twisting her hands in front of her in silent anguish. 'Let's keep calm if we can. Have you looked for it carefully?'

'Of course I have. I put it in the top left-hand drawer, which has a lock. The point is that after we had coffee yesterday morning I forgot to lock it. I didn't go back to lock the drawer until late last night and then I didn't bother to check that the file was still there. I assumed it would be.'

'But I've searched them and the room. It's gone and we don't have to look far to find out who's stolen it.'

'I didn't,' Rowan protested again, but he remained unmoved by her entreaties. 'It could have been anyone. Someone from outside,' she suggested in desperation. This was like a nightmare; it just couldn't be happening.

'No one has broken in,' Damon said in that same detached voice that threatened to break her heart. 'And no one else had a reason or an opportunity. It would be too much of a coincidence for someone from the outside to know I had it here. I told no one I was bringing it home. Is that why you were down here last night when I came back? Did I disturb you? Or did you take it while we were getting ready for the dance?' Rowan shook her head. 'No wonder you were in such a good mood last night. You really had a good time, didn't you? All the time you had the file. It must have been very amusing for you. When I think . . . '

He started towards her and Laura said quickly, 'I can't believe it, Damon. Let's try and be reasonable.'

Abruptly, Damon turned on his sister. 'Reasonable! I know you dislike unpleasantness, Laura, but this is ridiculous. Don't you realise what it means? That report contained facts which, if used by a rival company, could cost us the patent to FU970, and we won't be able to do a thing about it. Years of research and money — your money and my work, Laura — will be gone — into the pocket of Louis Patrick.'

'Laura,' Rowan pleaded, 'tell him it wasn't me. I don't know what happened to his report. I only know that I didn't take it.'

Laura looked bewildered, too. She couldn't dispute the facts and yet she was obviously reluctant to disbelieve Rowan.

Damon shook his finger at her. She averted her eyes because she couldn't bear to look at him any longer, to see the anger he felt towards her.

'I'll give you one last chance to tell me. You either tell me or the police. It's up to you. Has it been posted off? They'll find out. It's amazing what the police can find out, and even if they do recover the file I'll still press charges against you. Louis Patrick's not the only man capable of being vindictive.'

'You are being vindictive,' she cried. 'You just want a chance to get back at him.'

'You can't transfer the blame to me. There's only one person in this house who would have reason to take that file. Now, tell me where it is. I'll beat it out of you if I have to.'

'Damon!' Laura cried. 'I've never seen you like this. For goodness sake keep control of your temper.'

But Damon was not listening. Laura might not have been there. 'Tell me,' he insisted. 'Don't think a few beguiling kisses can help you now. I'm over that madness. This has been too much a part of me to let go so easily, so you'd better tell me. I mean to know.'

Hamish, aware of the excitement, ran to and fro, barking wildly. All Rowan was able to do was shake her head. He looked at Laura. 'Stay here with her. I'm going to search her room before I call the police. There's a good chance that she still has it and I want to get it back as soon as I can.'

With one last scathing look at her he hurried from the room and she could hear him taking the stairs two at a time.

It was a hot day with a cloudless sky and not a breath of wind. Rowan had put on a sleeveless silk shift which had seemed sufficient, but now she was cold, desperately cold, and she clasped her arms around her body in an attempt to stop the shivering. She sank down on to the edge of the desk and made no attempt to stem the tears that gushed down her cheeks.

Laura took two hesitant steps forward. 'Rowan, tell me, oh, forgive me . . . I must know. Did you? Did you take that file?'

Rowan looked up sharply, her eyes filled with pain as well as tears. 'Oh, no, Laura, not you, too.'

She pushed past her and ran out into the hall. Hamish sprang up and bounded after her. Chris was just coming in, and to his astonishment, sobbing as she went, she pushed past him, too. She wrenched open the door to her car which had been standing outside, only to find that the keys weren't there; they were still in her room.

With tears coursing down her cheeks, Rowan got out again to find herself face to face with Chris. He was frowning, searching her face with anxious eyes.

'What in heaven's name is wrong?'

'Bring her inside, Chris,' Laura told

him from the doorway. 'There's been some trouble.'

Rowan brushed the tears away from her cheeks. When Chris put his hands on her shoulders, she tore away. 'Leave me be, Chris. Let me alone.'

She pulled away from him and, sobbing again, she began to run down the path. She had no idea where she was running, where she would go, but the urge to get away was strong in her. She wanted to run on and never go back, never to see the disgust and anger on his face again. She could bear anything but that; the anger and the total coldness towards her.

Behind him, Hamish's barking almost drowned the sound of Chris and Laura shouting her name over and over again, but she did not heed them. She kept on running, not even noticing where she was going.

Gradually her pace, of necessity, slowed. Rowan could no longer hear anyone calling her name. She didn't know where she was going. The path she had unconsciously taken led her upwards. She stumbled off the path, through conifers, over smooth turf and rough gorse. At last the trees were behind her and she sank down on to the heather out of sheer exhaustion.

The tears had dried on her face and her eyes felt heavy from all the tears she had shed. Her breath came in short gasps and an agonising pain stabbed into her side with the sharpness of a surgical knife.

She had no idea how long she had been walking, for when she glanced at her watch it had stopped. She put her head in her hands and gave a half-hysterical laugh; people spent their holidays walking these fells. She could understand why; it was such beautiful country. But Rowan never wanted to see this beautiful, lonely, heart-breaking country again. This country was Damon Halstead. Damon, whose kisses had promised her the world, whose distrust had given her only a misery that could never end.

Who had taken the file? she asked herself. Damon was right; no one else but herself would have a use for it. But his condemnation, his refusal to believe her denial, was unbearably painful.

The way she had fled from the house must confirm her guilt to him. Possibly already the police were out looking for her. Once more the names of Patrick and Halstead would be linked in scandal. The thought of it did not hurt her as much as the change in his attitude towards her. In a typically female way, that was all that mattered. As for the other, no one could prove she had stolen the file when she hadn't, but her heart ached unbearably at the thought that all his work would come to nothing — for the acclaim to go to another unjustly — and for Damon to hate her for it for the rest of his days.

She had climbed high up into the fells. The countryside spread out in a beautiful panorama around her, but for once she had no eye for its charm.

Misery surrounded her like an impenetrable blanket that blocked out all else.

'I couldn't have meant anything to him,' she said to herself, and unable to bear the thought she buried her head in her arms and cried heartbrokenly.

At last she fell into an uneasy sleep and when she awoke the sun was no longer blazing down on her. A chill wind had sprung up, drawing dark clouds across the sky like sailboats seeking a harbour.

Rowan sat up sharply. It was getting dark, although her senses told her it was still only afternoon. She shivered as the wind penetrated the thin silk of her dress and whipped her hair in front of her eyes.

She scrambled to her feet and looked around, desperately seeking a familiar landmark, but there was none. She was high up. The crags that loomed all around had taken on a menacing look, outlined eerily against the darkening sky. She flinched as a flicker of lightning momentarily lit up the horizon. The wind was growing so strong that she was finding it difficult to stand up straight.

When a rumble of thunder came out of the distance she began to run. Surely there must be a cottage nearby, she thought. People live around here. There must be somewhere I can shelter.

The wind tore frienziedly at her clothes as she stumbled off in the direction from which she had come. It was incredible how cold it had become. The blazing heat of the sun was just a memory. Like everything else, it had belonged to a different age; another life.

Another fork of lightning illuminated the sky, followed moments later by a crack of thunder that was almost deafening. Hadn't Chris warned her about the ferocious storms that usually followed idyllic weather? And she had said she wanted her visit to end with a big bang!

She had reached a belt of trees. The wind was roaring through them, forcing them to bow in its path, and they groaned and creaked at the effort. A few spots of rain started down and Rowan halted breathlessly under a tree as hailstones, the size of marbles, began to beat down. She huddled under the tree, which gave no shelter as the hail pounded into her mercilessly, and she cried out loud as they stung her bare arms and legs.

She clung on to the tree trunk for fear that the wind would sweep her away. Its branches threshed in torment above her head. The hail was turning to torrential rain, which was hardly more kind to her battered body. As she stood, almost petrified, she watched the ground turn to mud in moments. Lightning forked in front of her eyes and a branch crashed to the ground at her feet. Her terrified scream was drowned by the roar of the thunder and the wind.

Hardly knowing what she was doing, Rowan tore herself away from the trees and it was blind terror that forced her on. As she ran, her feet gave way beneath her and she sank, ankle deep, into mud. There was no shelter to be had. Not a light shone out of the darkness to give her hope.

She was too frightened to know where she was going, or what she was doing. Through the nightmare of driving rain and the storm's onslaught on her senses, Rowan realised that she was running downhill, steeply. The path, if it was one, was a sea of slippery mud and several times she fell, and on each occasion it took all her willpower to drag herself up again.

Her senses told her it was only minutes since the storm began, yet it might have been going on for hours. She was cold and soaked and bruised, and she felt that she just couldn't go on any further. As she peered ahead she could see nothing but driving rain. She was completely lost and without hope.

In her despair and fear she stumbled, ankle deep, into a small beck. As she backed out, sobbing and fighting against the might of the storm, a flash of lightning and a crack of thunder came almost simultaneously, bringing down small boulders from the crags above. The wind came like a giant hand and pitched her back into the water, and along with the loosened boulders Rowan was being swept helplessly down the hillside into a morass of oblivion.

*   *   *

There was something moist against her cheek. Someone was breathing hoarsely near by. The wind that sighed through the trees sounded as if it were singing a lullaby. Rowan could hardly believe the terrible onslaught was over. She tried to open her eyes, but there was only darkness and wetness and someone breathing near by.

'Good boy, Hamish!' a distant voice cried. 'Good boy. You've found her!'

The voice sounded like Damon's, but it could have been Chris's. Their voices were similar and she was very confused. Hamish began to bark.

'Good grief!' It was Chris. 'Just look at her. If she's alive it will be a miracle.'

'She'd better be. She'd better be.'

It was Damon. She recognised his voice now it was closer. It was thick as if he'd been shouting, or choked with emotion.

She let out a sigh, but it sounded very much like a groan.

'All right, darling. You're all right now. We're going to take you back now. Does anything hurt badly?'

'Everything,' she managed to say, opening her eyes and then closing them against the harsh glare of the lights all around.

'She doesn't seem too bad,' he said a moment later. 'I don't think there's any broken bones. We'll have to risk it.' She hated the way he was talking over her. It was as if she were not there — dead perhaps. 'Here, take my torch, Chris, while I lift her. Someone had better tell the others we've found her.'

'Damon,' she said as he lifted her gently.

'Don't say anything just now, Rowan.'

'I didn't take your file. I want you to believe me in case I die. I didn't take it.'

'You're not going to die. And I know you didn't take the file. Relax now. I'm taking you back.'

★   ★   ★

Her dreams were all terrifying ones. In one she dreamt that Laura and Mrs Jennings were trying to drown her and were being apologetic about it. But when she awoke it was to a feeling of peace. Sunlight shone through a chink in the curtains. It was as if that biblical onslaught had never been. She moved and winced with pain. Her fingers explored her body gingerly and found only tenderness and sticking-plaster.

The door opened a crack and Rowan said, 'Come in, Laura.'

'How do you feel?' Laura asked, coming into the room. Her brow was furrowed with anxiety.

'I hurt all over. What's the diagnosis?'

'Dr McAllister says you're suffering from no more than bruises and mild exposure. He's left some tablets if you're very sore. Did you rest well?'

'Like the dead. After that experience, who wouldn't? It was like being caught in the jaws of hell.'

Laura drew the curtains apart slightly to reveal clear blue sky. 'Who would ever have thought . . . ' Rowan murmured.

'No one realises how bad it can be out there. Every year, even in the height of summer, people are hurt and lost in those storms. Every year search parties have to go out. Sometimes they're not found until it's too late . . . '

'How long have I been here?'

'Since last night. You were gone all afternoon and when the storm came we knew you'd be in trouble, so the men organised the usual search parties. Damon, Robert and Chris are always on call. The boys know this area well. So do most of the locals.' She took a deep breath. 'Anyway, you were found quite soon, thank goodness. You didn't have to spend the night out there, which is a mercy. But you were in an awful mess, Rowan. I nearly passed out when they brought you in. You were covered in mud and slime. Mrs Jennings and I had to bath you to uncover the damage. There's not a part of you that isn't bruised. Dr McAllister says you're to stay in bed for a day or two to recover.'

She moved away from the window. She seemed oddly uncomfortable. Rowan said, 'When will the police want to talk to me, Laura?'

'Police? They weren't called. Rescue operations aren't mounted by the police. They're organised locally unless it's to be very intensive. Fortunately we found you with just local help.'

'I didn't mean about that. About the file on FU970.'

Laura's finger traced the pattern on the bed head. 'You don't have to worry about that any more. It's turned up. We'll talk about it later. You must rest now.'

She started towards the door and Rowan said, 'Just a minute, Laura. Damon isn't the type of man just to misplace a file as important as this one.'

Laura was unable to meet Rowan's eye. 'He didn't. Carolyne took it.'

'Carolyne!' Rowan winced as she moved. 'That doesn't make sense. Why should Carolyne take something that belonged to her father's firm?'

'I wish you hadn't asked right now, but seeing you have, I may as well tell you; she took it with the vague idea of discrediting you, an idea that worked only too well. When she heard what had happened to you she confessed immediately, returned it and insisted on joining the search party. It was simply done in a fit of female pique.

'She's spoiled, you know. Really spoiled. She's always thought she could do anything. This has brought her up with a shock. She's realised the damage she can do when she only half tries.'

'I've no need to tell you how

ashamed she is, or how ashamed we all are.'

She smiled, albeit tightly, for the first time since entering the room. 'Rest now, dear, and we'll talk later. You've nothing to worry about now.'

The door closed behind her and Rowan sank back into the pillows. '*Nothing to worry about now.*'

How ironic. Whatever might have come of her love for Damon, was now finished and Laura could say, 'You've nothing to worry about now.'

Rowan pressed her face into the pillow, laughed jerkily, and slept.

★ ★ ★

When she awoke it was to see Laura again. She was standing next to the bed, carrying a tray.

'I've brought you some lunch,' she said, her face now wearing a bright smile. 'I didn't know what to bring, so I thought steamed fish and creamed potatoes would be easiest for you. You won't want anything too heavy just now.'

Rowan smiled as she struggled to sit up. 'That will be fine, Laura.'

Laura settled on the edge of the bed as Rowan made an heroic attempt to eat. 'Your father's on his way here.'

Rowan looked up at her, her eyes wide and disbelieving. 'Daddy is coming *here?*'

Laura nodded. 'We've received a telegram as long as a letter. It must have cost him a fortune to send.'

'But he was on a yacht in the Aegean . . . '

'He chartered a couple of planes, I believe. He's arriving sometime today.'

'Laura, he couldn't possibly have known about yesterday. No one contacted him, surely.'

'He knows nothing about your accident. I dread to think what he'll say when he does find out. He'll be furious and we deserve his anger.'

'It seems that your boyfriend contacted him on the radio telephone. He told him all about Delia's will, you being here, and that you showed no disposition to leave. He must have put into port immediately.'

Rowan sank back in to the pillows. 'I don't want him here. There's been enough trouble already . . .'

'Oh, dear, it's all such a mess,' said Laura in a tremulous voice.

'Where's Damon?' asked Rowan boldly. It was the one question, above all others, that she'd been aching to ask, but hadn't dared until now.

Laura brushed her hair back from her shiny forehead. 'He's gone out — to the factory, to put that file under lock and key, I imagine. He's had little chance until now.

'I wish he'd never brought it home at all. He can't have really believed you'd take it or he wouldn't have brought it home. He's not at all absentminded. Try to look at it that way, Rowan. You can't really blame him for jumping to the most obvious conclusion.'

'I'm not blaming him, Laura.'

'He's probably working right now. It won't be the first time he's worked alone on a Sunday. And although it's unlike him, I suppose he's not at all anxious to face you.'

Rowan put her fork down after taking only a few mouthfuls. 'Aren't you eating any more?' Laura asked.

'I can't.'

Laura removed the tray and looked so worried that Rowan said gently, 'Laura, if you look in the wardrobe you'll find the painting of the Hall I did for you. It's finished.'

Laura did as Rowan asked. She drew the painting out carefully. 'It's wonderful,' she cried after a moment.

'Well, if you don't like it you can always consign it to the attic. It might be discovered by some future Halstead and be acclaimed as a masterpiece in about a hundred years.'

'I'll do nothing of the kind! There's no need. It's a lovely painting. It has ... atmosphere. Oh, I did want to make up for everything, Rowan, and just look what's happened instead!'

Rowan frowned. 'Make up for what, Laura?'

Laura drew a sigh and propped the painting against the wall. 'For everything that happened. Having Delia, for another thing. I often thought about it — you alone with that man and us a whole family. Robert always says I'm too sensitive, but I can't help it. Now it's all turned into a disaster.'

'Don't feel that way, Laura,' Rowan answered gently. She was touched by the woman's concern. 'There's been a little unpleasantness, but mostly I've had a lovely time.' She hesitated a moment before adding, 'You're a rare person, Laura, and I'm very happy to know you. You've got to come to London with Robert next time he's on business there and we'll go out on the town. We'll have a marvellous time together. I insist that you come. You will, won't you?'

Laura beamed. 'Yes, we will. I am glad you're not angry with me.'

'It never occurred to me, Laura. I'm very angry with myself, though. I should have known my coming here would cause trouble.'

Laura took the tray. 'I'll leave you to rest for a while. Dr McAllister says that is all you need.'

When Laura had gone, Rowan drew a deep sigh. Her father's coming must be the last act in this little drama. Rowan pulled back the covers. Those parts of her which weren't covered with plaster were a mass of bruises and grazes. It took some effort for her to get out of bed. Every part of her ached. She dressed slowly and with considerable difficulty, but managed it at last. Then she threw all of her belongings into her suitcase and snapped shut the locks.

Daddy was coming, and that could only mean trouble. She intended, quite literally, to be waiting on the doorstep, ready to leave, the moment he arrived. Apart from that, there was a cowardly voice inside her head telling her she must not see Damon again, for if she did her precarious self-control would break down.

He was proud and he had been proved wrong. Nothing could now come of what was begun between them such a short time ago. Mistrust had killed it and pride would prevent it being reborn, yet the memory of that short period of delight would remain with her for ever. She loved him despite his failure to trust her. In his place, Rowan doubted if she would have acted differently.

Her hand almost froze to the stair rail when Carolyne came into the hall. She had been making her way down the stairs and every step hurt. The sight of Carolyne moving lithely caused resentment to stir again. But when she drew closer the girl's face was so sombre and her eyes red from the tears she had shed, Rowan could no longer maintain that feeling.

'May I speak to you?' she asked in a small voice, without looking directly at Rowan.

'I can't stop you,' she answered, limping across to the sitting room.

'Please, just a few minutes.' She followed Rowan into the sitting room. 'I don't blame you for feeling this way. You have every reason to hate me for what I did, but please believe me when I say I'm sorry.'

Rowan, rather than risk the discomfort of sitting, remained on her feet. 'Why don't you sit down?' she asked Carolyne, and the girl did so, giving her a ghost of a smile at the same time.

'I was surprised to see you up. You looked terrible last night. Are you feeling all right?'

'I'm coming to the conclusion that I will survive,' Rowan answered drily.

'You can joke about it. I wish I could. I wish you'd be angry with me. It would be better.'

'There's no point. You've apologised and I accept.'

Rowan turned to look out of the window. The sun was shining; the water was golden, and it was a beautiful day again. Not a sign of that terrible storm could be seen.

'You're too kind, much too kind,' Carolyne said in a rush. Rowan felt uncomfortable. She didn't like to see Carolyne Griffin humble herself, whatever she'd done. 'You might consider you've had a lucky escape, but I've been luckier.' Rowan turned to look at her. 'If anything really bad had happened to you I'd have had it on my conscience for the rest of my life. I think I've escaped better than I deserve.'

'Well,' Rowan answered with a smile, 'I'm certainly not going to get myself lost again just to satisfy your masochistic urges.'

'I didn't plan anything. It wasn't done with deliberate malice; I want you to know that, Miss Patrick. It was an impulse. I just wanted you to go from here.'

'You've been successful; I'm leaving today.'

Carolyne lowered her eyes. 'That day, after you came, I was with Damon when Josh Naylor told him. He was furious. He said he thought you'd come to ferret out what information you could about the drug he was working on. Then when I saw you with Chris . . . Well, I told myself it was for the firm's sake.'

'You were jealous over Chris.'

She sighed. 'Yes, I suppose so. I felt so bad when you were lost — frightened too — but it was even worse when Chris told me you'd tried to make things right between us; that you'd sensed what we couldn't admit to ourselves and you'd made him aware of it. I was in love with Chris once, but he was always so casual about me. I was afraid of being hurt. I told myself I didn't love him and that Damon would never treat me badly. I'm fond of Damon, but . . . '

'I hope things will go right between you now,' Rowan told her, and she was being sincere.

'Yes, I believe you do. But I don't know now. He was so angry with me, and I don't blame him. I'm not the most popular person around here today. Damon gave me an earful, too. Of course, it's all over between us now, not that it was more than luke-warm at best. If Chris still wants to, then I'm willing to try. We shall have to see.'

'I'm sure he won't be angry with you for long. Will you stay and have some tea with me before I go?'

Carolyne got to her feet quickly. 'No, thank you. I didn't come to stay. I have a new pupil starting this afternoon, so I must go.' She went towards the door. 'I really am glad you're all right, and it's good of you to be so forgiving. You've relieved my mind a great deal. Good-bye.'

'Good luck, Carolyne.'

After she had gone, Rowan limped across to the table and helped herself to a cigarette. She rarely smoked, but with her ears straining for the arrival of her father she needed something to do.

She had only just lit the cigarette when Laura came bustling into the room in a great fluster. 'Did I see Carolyne leaving just now?'

'She came to apologise. She was most humble.'

Laura drew herself up indignantly. 'I should think so. Now, what are you doing down here? Dr McAllister said . . .'

'I know what Dr McAllister said, but I'm going to avoid any more unpleasantness, Laura. I'm leaving the moment my father arrives. It's the best thing.'

Laura looked as if she would like to say something but didn't know quite what. Rowan crushed out the cigarette. 'Laura, when Damon comes tell him . . . will you tell him . . . ?'

'Oh, tell him yourself,' she said airily. 'If I'm not mistaken, he's here now.'

Rowan stiffened and then clasped her arms around her body to stop herself trembling. Laura opened the door and as Damon came in she went out.

'What are you doing down here?' he demanded.

It was typical of him. He was still being arrogant.

'Haven't you been told . . . ?'

'I'm leaving. My father's coming for me and I'm leaving with him immediately. I should have gone days ago. If I had, all the trouble would have been avoided.'

The mask of arrogance seemed to fall from his face, to be replaced by an expression of concern. He came up to her, which was a threat to her careful composure. 'How are you? Do you hurt very much?'

'More than you'd ever believe, Damon.'

'What can I say to you?'

'Nothing.' She gave a feeble little laugh. 'Whatever else you do, don't apologise. Everyone seems intent on apologising this morning, and I've had quite enough of it. I'm grateful to you, actually, for finding me so soon. Did I look awful?' she asked lightly.

Surprisingly he smiled. 'Like you'd been embalmed in mud, and your dress was torn to shreds.'

She smiled, too. 'I'm glad I didn't know about it; it might have been embarrassing.'

His smile faded. 'You can't imagine the agonies I suffered when you were lost in that storm, and it was all because I leapt to a conclusion. I treated you abominably, Rowan. I wish I knew a way of making it up to you, for all I said, the pain I caused. If there is any way, you must let me know. I'll do anything.'

She searched his face for a long moment. Breathlessly she asked, 'Do you really mean that?'

'I've never meant anything more.'

'Then tell me; the night of the dance when we were here together, did you mean all those things you said to me?'

A shadow of pain passed across his face. 'I meant everything.'

'Then mean it again, Damon,' she begged.

He looked at her incredulously and then he caught hold of her arms. 'After what happened?'

She winced beneath his grip, but the pain did not seem to matter. 'It makes no difference. You believed what you were meant to believe.'

He kissed her gently and her arms went around his neck.

'I thought you'd want to leave here for good after all that's happened. I thought you'd never want to see us again, and I thought it best to let you go.'

'You have no idea what is best.'

'I didn't want to believe it was you, Rowan, but there seemed no other answer. After I was so hasty in condemning you at first, I would have given anything to take it all back.'

'You did — the other night.'

'It wasn't soon enough, only I thought there might be something between you and Chris and it was simply jealousy that kept me from saying something to you earlier.'

'No more apologies, Damon. Never again.'

'Would you even be willing to marry me?' he asked.

'If you're asking me.'

'I am. I intended to yesterday, but it's been delayed for twenty-four hours while I went through hell.'

'That makes two of us, and I'm not just talking about my being lost out there, but it doesn't matter now. You'll just have to handle me gently for the moment.'

He smiled. 'That might be rather difficult.'

'Then that will have to be your punishment.'

'You couldn't devise a worse one.' The smile faded. 'Rowan, your father will be furious.'

She giggled. 'Yes, won't he just.' At the realisation that Damon was really anxious, she became serious again. 'He's not so alarming,' she added. 'He'll come to understand.'

When a car drew up outside she knew he had arrived. She could hear his voice shouting orders to the driver before he even reached the door. When Louis Patrick was around, there were few who didn't know it.

For a moment she knew alarm. How would they fare, these two men she loved? Two men who had quick, furious tempers and an implacable stubbornness; and there were two decades of bitterness between.

Damon put his arm around her. 'He's going to get quite a shock any minute now, but don't worry, darling, I'll treat him gently.'

With a contented smile, she laid her head on Damon's shoulder and as they went to greet her father Rowan knew there would be no more trouble. The clouds had gone from the valley for good.

THE END

We do hope that you have enjoyed reading this large print book.

Did you know that all of our titles are available for purchase?

We publish a wide range of high quality large print books including:
Romances, Mysteries, Classics
General Fiction
Non Fiction and Westerns

Special interest titles available in large print are:
The Little Oxford Dictionary
Music Book, Song Book
Hymn Book, Service Book

Also available from us courtesy of Oxford University Press:
Young Readers' Dictionary
(large print edition)
Young Readers' Thesaurus
(large print edition)

For further information or a free brochure, please contact us at:
Ulverscroft Large Print Books Ltd.,
The Green, Bradgate Road, Anstey,
Leicester, LE7 7FU, England.
Tel: (00 44) **0116 236 4325**
Fax: (00 44) **0116 234 0205**